Dry SPELL

Sweet Escape Series – Book One

MIA LONDON & SUSAN SHEEHEY

AMEPPHIRE PRESS

Dry Spell
Sweet Escape Series
Book One
by Mia London and Susan Sheehey

ISBN: 978-1947874107 (E-Book)
978-1947874138 (paperback)

Publisher: Amepphire Press
11923 NE Sumner St, Ste 766015
Portland, OR 97220

Edited by Traci Hall
Formatted by Formatting by Leigh
Cover design copyright © L.J. Anderson, Mayhem Cover Creations

Published in the United States of America

Dedication
TO OUR HUSBANDS

Because if they have no idea what we're doing,

they pretend like they do, and support us

anyway.

Other novels
BY MIA & SUSAN

Other Novels by Mia London & Susan Sheehey

Dry Spell

Hot Spell

Cold Spell

Other Novels by Mia London

Undeniable Series

Undeniable Fate

Undeniable Love

Perfect Series

Perfect Seduction

Perfect Surrender

Life To The Max

Wanton Angel *(Prequel to Life To The Max)*

Beyond Lace (Hard Men of the Rockies 4)

Other Novels by Susan Sheehey

Royals of Solana Series

Prince of Solana

Jewel of Solana

Crown of Solana

Royal Wedding novella

Knights of Texas Series

Tell Me What You Want

Tell Me What You Crave

Tell Me What You Need

Tell Me What You Feel

Audrey's Promise

SAMANTHA CALLAHAN SLAMMED the lid closed on her laptop. *The most* satisfying sound known to mankind. Who would ever use a tablet when the closing of a lid felt so final . . . so complete?

She smiled for the first time in three days. Her project was finished and, glancing at the clock, with thirty minutes to spare. Her boss would see it first thing in the morning, and love it, of course. Next, nail the presentation and get one step closer to her promotion.

I'm at the top of my game.

Time to celebrate.

She reached into the fridge for one of her favorite California whites. After a generous pour, she hammered the cork back into place with her fist, and strode to her living room to binge on Netflix. In the distance, outside her living room window, the Golden Gate Bridge gleamed with spotlights illuminating the suspension cables, despite a thin layer of fog.

The same view she'd loved when she'd toured this

apartment six years ago, and the deciding factor in signing the lease. But as she huddled into the couch with her overfilled glass of wine, she couldn't remember the last time she'd looked out the window. Work was her obsession.

Only a few minutes into the first episode, her cell phone chimed. She ignored it until she heard it again. Sam glanced at the screen. An email from her boss. Something about scheduling a meeting with the client to close the deal.

Instead of reading his more-than-likely verbose critique on her little screen, she grabbed her laptop from the coffee table.

Sam's boss was an even bigger control freak than her. But after this proposal, she was certain he'd have no choice but to let her run point for this new client. Thereby, earning that coveted new director role.

Finally, I have my chance.

The second she opened the lid, the computer screen flashed an ugly blue.

Samantha's heart froze. A gasp lodged in her throat.

The blue screen of death.

Her life was on that computer. Her project proposal, her presentation, all her sales leads . . .

No matter how many times she pressed the escape button, or control-alt-delete, nothing worked. Until the little black bar in the center popped up.

Deleting files...

"No!" she screamed, lunging forward. Her wine spilled

all over the keyboard. The subtle lights under the keys flickered, then died.

Her computer shut off, the hard drive's faint hum dwindling into silence.

Oh God, no. This cannot be happening.

She smashed her lips together, and inhaled through her nostrils. *Think.*

She opened her email on her phone, and all her messages were still there. No crisis. *Thank God.*

She could fix this. All she needed to do was take it in to the computer nerds. They could fix anything. This wasn't the first time the geniuses had to fix the blue screen of death for someone, and it certainly wouldn't be the last. This would be easy to repair, right?

At least that's what she kept telling herself.

Sam grabbed a towel from the kitchen, blotted what she could, and turned her laptop upside down to let any remaining wine drip out.

She stood with hands on her hips, mourning her beloved laptop. *Well, that's just great.*

DON'T DRINK AND drive goes for computer work as well." The repair guy snorted at his own joke. Far too ornery on a Friday morning for Sam's tastes.

She glowered. *Comedian of the century, this one.* "It was an *accident.*"

"It always is. Here's the important question," he sighed behind his black-rimmed glasses. "Did you backup your data?"

"Of course, I did . . . " She scoured her mind for the last time she'd synced up her external hard drive. Her heart sank. "Last Christmas."

Trevor, from his nametag, audibly winced. "You need to do that more often—"

"I know," she barked back, then bit her tongue. "I'm sorry. There's just a lot of important stuff on this hard drive. Can you save that?"

"Maybe. We won't know until we get in there and poke around. Give us until next week."

She blinked. "Next week?"

"We're pretty slammed, and it's a holiday weekend."

Of course it is. Shit!

He entered her contact information and passwords, and followed with, "We'll give you a call." That was it. What more could she do?

She released a breath and headed to the car.

At her car door, she let the cool air calm her heated face. A warm breeze blew, chasing off the fog across the bay, allowing thin sunbeams to dance across the water's surface. The radio forecast had hinted at a warm front coming this week, and tourists were sure to flock to San Francisco. Mocking her current dismal situation. She wanted to crawl under a rock and die.

The nerd's words replayed in her head. *You need to do that more often.*

A little late for that.

You're a smart woman, Sam. In thirty years, you've learned nothing?

Before she could berate herself any further, her phone rang. The screen displayed "Jordan Beck," her best friend, along with her picture, reminiscent of a smiling Mila Kunis.

"Hey, Jordan. This really isn't—"

"Morning, sunshine. With you, it's never a good time. But we love you anyway."

God, she was more chipper than usual. "Morning. What's up?"

"Guess what?" Jordan didn't wait for a reply. Her excitement about something sizzled over the car speakers. "I found us an incredible deal on a beach house in Santa Cruz for the week. A last minute cancellation, and we're taking advantage."

Her eyes narrowed on the display screen in her car. *Was this really her BFF talking?* "For a *week*? Are you crazy?"

"Nope. *You're* crazy because you work too damn much. Your boss *wants* you to take a break. How much vacation time do you have accumulated, Sam? Ten years? And it's Fourth of July weekend, in case you've forgotten."

Actually, she had. Nerd had to remind her.

"So, get your bikini and toothbrush, and be outside

your place in two hours."

What?! "You cannot be serious, Jordan."

"Like a heart attack. Liddy is already on board. We'll work on our tans, shop, snorkel, flirt with the hotties, and dance our asses off. So, pack your bag." Jordan was adamant.

Sam let out an exasperated sigh. Really, she had no good reason to stay home. Any meeting with the client would be at least a week or two away, and certainly not over the holiday. Besides, a dead computer meant work would have to wait.

Did she want to miss this trip? Her last beach vacation had been eons ago. Sam had even missed Christmas with her parents because of a big presentation for another new client worth twice her salary, which she'd nailed, of course.

She was justifying.

Her sigh felt like an anvil on her shoulders. "I don't know, Jordan."

"Perfect. See you in one hour fifty-eight minutes." The line went dead.

Shit!

Chapter TWO

GET YOUR NOSE out of your phone, and look *up*, Sam," Liddy chuckled from the front seat. Her giddy, cherub-like face should've been contagious, but Sam still wallowed over her destroyed laptop from the backseat of Jordan's car.

When she'd called her boss to ask for the time off, he didn't hesitate. He'd loved her presentation, and she'd more than earned it.

"Go ahead, live it up. About time you had a break," he'd said.

She glanced up, and raised her eyebrows.

The beach house spread before her was an adorable, quaint stucco home with a brown tile roof, and light blue shutters. The drive circled around a lush flower bed with a tall, oversized palm tree providing a canopy over the front entrance. But what caught her attention the most was the ocean view behind it. Through the windows straight to the back of the house shimmered a calm sea. A handful of people already sat on the beach or swam in the water, a picturesque image worthy of a postcard.

"Wow," they said in unison.

"We're staying here?" Liddy's voice went up an octave at the last word. She pulled her platinum blonde hair back from her face, and leaned forward in her seat.

"Yup. This is ours for a week, girls."

Even Sam had to admit, a place like this would make anyone forget their troubles.

"Okay, everyone grab a bag," Jordan said.

The trio had stopped on the way to buy groceries for the week. They carried in bags containing coffee, chicken, hamburgers, apples, chocolate, and God knew what else. Frankly, Sam had been distracted with thoughts of her dead PC and what excuse she could come up with to get her ass back to San Fran.

"Ah!" Sam heard Liddy's yell from inside the house.

She dropped her luggage and ran inside.

"What is it?" Jordan called.

"Look at this deck. It's huge. And this beach! It's like our own private paradise."

Sam and Liddy crossed the ginormous living room furnished with two sofas, two arm chairs, a few tables, and a flat-screen TV mounted on the wall. They walked through the open doorway out to the back deck. The view was breathtaking. Sam wanted to capture the blue of the water and bring it back with her to replace the grayish-green of San Francisco Bay.

Liddy squealed again and clapped her hands.

"You think she'd never seen sand before," Sam muttered to Jordan before going back to unload the car.

EVERYONE ON THE beach in ten minutes," Jordan announced as she finished unpacking the groceries. "Including you, Sam." She pulled the phone from Sam's hands and shoved it in a drawer. "Go get your suit on. Your body will thank me for the vitamin D it's starving for."

Sam leaned her hip on the counter. "You thrive on controlling everything, don't you?"

Jordan threw her a wink. "Admit it. You like someone else taking the reins for a while. Otherwise, you'd go cross-eyed staring at computer and phone screens your whole life. As your best friend, it's my job to make sure you have some fun. Now, scoot."

She huffed, and dragged her hastily-packed bag upstairs. Vacations were overrated, and caused huge dents in people's schedules. With this one-week getaway, Sam would have to spend the next month catching up. Just in time to see her career zooming by.

The nautical themed bedroom was meant to be relaxing, but the navy curtains and a sailboat painting over the double-sized bed simply annoyed her.

"Such a cliché," she muttered. Even the anchor-shaped handles on the white-washed dresser and armoire matched the bed lamps.

She tossed her bag on the bed and went through the items she'd managed to throw inside in her one-hour packing spree. Unpacking would be a waste of time, since Sam didn't plan on staying—even if she had to Uber back. But she unloaded anyway, carefully hanging up her shirts and pants, and one dress. Bathing-wear was easy because she only had one suit—a salmon-colored bikini she'd bought senior year of college, and hadn't worn since.

"Two minute warning," Jordan called from downstairs.

Samantha sighed and slipped on her bikini, nearly swallowing her tongue when she saw her reflection in the mirror.

"Did this thing shrink?" Her way-too-accentuated cleavage terrified her. There was so much more exposed than she remembered.

Shit! She grabbed her cover-up and threw it on.

At the bottom of the stairs, Jordan waited in an adorable black sports bikini with white daisies embroidered across the hem. Tan, tone, and perfect bust size.

Unlike me . . . I'm spilling out like the Pillsbury Doughboy.

"Muumuu off. You need some sun."

Sam glared. "It's a cover-up, and I agreed to come along at the last minute. Stop pushing me."

Her friend threw up her hands dramatically and turned to the patio sliding door.

The warm salty breeze hit her face, and her annoyance at the trip vanished. She'd forgotten that smell. Fresh and flowery. Not like San Francisco's musty fog, with a hint of stale urine.

"This is what I'm talking about." Jordan waved at Liddy, already on the beach and lathering sunscreen on her arms—she looked fantastic in a green bikini with thin straps crisscrossing her bust, which worked fabulously on her thin frame.

Sam was so envious. To have a body that slender? Maybe her previous relationship wouldn't have ended so badly.

The second her feet hit the warm sand, she smiled. The granules massaged between her toes, soft and smooth. *Better than a pedicure.*

Only a handful of people enjoyed the beach today—a couple, two families, a small group farther up the way, and two surfers.

Sam popped the top off her sunscreen and began covering any possible exposed skin. Blonde hair and blue eyes translated to "insta-scorch."

"Hot damn!" Liddy muttered.

Jordan whistled, long and slow.

Sam followed their stares.

A surfer out on the waves maneuvered in and out of the water, sometimes falling out of sight as he raced through the inside of the curl. He seemed to be very good. Probably lots of practice, from no job. Sam smirked.

After her body was well-coated in sunscreen, she offered some to Jordan. "You need any SPF50?"

Her friends' eyes remained glued to the surfer.

"Wow!" Jordan said.

Sam looked up in time to see the surfer jump a huge wave, holding his board with one hand, the other arm out for balance—followed by a flawless landing.

Liddy pushed her wind-blown hair back from her eyes. "That guy's good."

"Mm-hmm," Jordan chimed in. "He looks like an Adonis."

"Ladies, would you like some sunscreen, or do you just want to burn while gawking?"

Jordan reached her hand to Sam haphazardly. "Sure, I'll take some."

The surfer swam closer to shore, giving the ladies a better vantage of his body. This sport certainly seemed to be good for building muscles. As he made his way inland, his shoulders and arms, and super-toned legs, were prominently displayed. Then he stood, wiped the water from his face, and lifted his surfboard.

Sam's heart skipped.

His abs had ridges she only saw on men in underwear ads. His arm muscles flexed as he walked on dry sand to his towel a short distance over. He drove his board into the sand to keep it standing, and even through his long swim trunks, his thigh muscles worked.

Shit! How could she be attracted to him? He wasn't even her type. Business suits, crisp shirts, and silk ties were more her preference.

Her friends still gawked.

Sam rolled her eyes, and reached for her paperback in her canvas bag.

"Afternoon ladies," Sam heard from overhead.

"Afternoon," Jordan replied.

Sam adjusted her sunglasses.

Surfer-boy stood at the foot of her towel. Sunlight glinted off his stunning cobalt irises, and nearly stole her breath. Until he smiled at her, and she silently gasped as he looked at her legs and overexposed skin.

She rose to her elbows and pulled at her cover-up, which had served as a pillow.

"Are you ladies renting this house?" He pointed at their mini beach mansion.

"Yes. Are you renting next door?" Jordan asked.

"No, I live there."

Seriously? Sam stole a glance at his house.

The same brown tile roof as theirs, with a white stone facade covered the back of the house. His espresso-colored deck held a covered seating area with a fire pit in the middle, surrounded by pistachio canvas curtains, and a shower head at the bottom of the steps.

He has excellent taste in decor.

She looked back to see him still watching her.

"You were pretty good out there. Have you been surfing long?" Liddy asked.

He broke eye contact with Sam long enough to look at Liddy.

Sam quickly lay her cover-up over her waist and hips. *Dear God, he's staring at my cellulite.*

"For a few years now. Do you ladies surf?" He turned his attention back to Sam.

She shook her head.

Jordan replied with a smile. "No, but maybe you could teach us."

The corner of his lips curved upward. "Maybe."

Sam fidgeted under his stare.

"Though, you'd probably fall out of those beautiful bikinis."

The girls laughed, but Sam looked skyward behind her sunglasses.

One of those *guys.*

"I'm Chase."

"This is Sam, I'm Jordan, and this is Liddy." Jordan motioned with her hand. "We're from San Francisco."

"Nice to meet you all. I need to get inside and wash off the saltwater. Enjoy your stay." He gave Sam a parting wink and headed back to his board.

"Holy mother of God. He is gorgeous," Jordan said in a loud whisper.

"Dripping wet or dry?" Liddy asked.

"Either way. I don't care." Jordan let out an audible sigh. "What's with you Sam? You didn't say a word."

"He was towering over me. What's with that?"

Liddy leaned forward to face Sam. "He only had eyes for you, Sam."

"Whatever," she mumbled.

"You need to learn to relax, sister. And get rid of the muumuu." Jordan grabbed the fabric across her waist, balled it up, and flung it in the water.

"Jordan!" Sam jumped up to retrieve her soaked garment and glanced out of the corner of her eye.

Surfer-boy chuckled before he walked toward his house.

Perfect! Can this be more humiliating?

She narrowed her eyes at Jordan and sat back down.

"Seriously, Sam. His eyes were all over you saying *let me show you what a real man can do.*"

Jordan had a one-track mind.

Her cover-up dripping with water, Sam wrung it out and dropped it on the corner of her towel. "So, I should just jump him?"

"What's wrong with a little vacation-sex?" Liddy joined the assault.

"Time to get that stick out of your vagina and replace it with a cock." Jordan smiled, and Liddy laughed.

"This was a big mistake."

"No, this is exactly what you need. What we all need. A distraction. A release, and plenty of eye candy."

"I'll drink to that," Liddy said as she opened the cooler and pulled out three beers.

Sam twisted off the cap and took a big swig. She needed to cool off. This might be one hell of a long week. She couldn't decide where she'd rather be—at home, worrying about her laptop, or on the beach with two crude matchmakers.

Liddy clanked her bottle again Jordan's, then reached toward Sam's. "To Jordan. Best idea ever."

Chapter THREE

WHEN CHASE HAD awoken that morning, he knew it was going to be a good day. The sun beamed, and based on the sound of the waves, the surf was ideal. The second he'd opened his eyes, he pulled up his phone app to check wind speed and swells. *Excellent!*

The temp was perfect, so he wouldn't need a wetsuit. And damn if his day didn't get even better.

Chase nearly drooled when he saw a Scarlett Johansson look-alike sunbathing on the sand. Those curves were Maxim-worthy, and he couldn't tear his eyes off her. But of the three women, she was the only one who hadn't smiled.

Makes me wonder what she looks like when she's not having fun.

At the beach, for Christ's sake. In a bikini that would have him kneeling at an altar with how damn hot she looked. Not too flashy or revealing, but left enough to a man's imagination. This Sam wore a bikini the way it was always meant to look.

Sam. The name was so abrupt and simple. But with her

blonde locks and curvy figure, her feminine form deserved a more fitting name, a softer moniker.

He'd stalled before he approached them. He'd had to get a handle on his libido. Clearly, appreciating her display was not meant for the world to see. Luckily, he could hide most of it behind his suit and towel.

He rinsed off in the shower on deck, scraping his hands through his hair to remove the excess salt. He needed a haircut, but who cared when he spent every afternoon surfing instead of stuck in a boardroom. Early retirement had its perks.

That Jordan woman was funny and direct, probably used to the spotlight. But Sam looked like she didn't want the attention. The most beautiful of the three, in his opinion, but the most standoffish. The woman had a lot of barriers set up around her psyche. He had a knack for reading people, and his gut told him, there was something more there . . .

He strolled inside and took a shower, then dressed in cargo shorts and a loose short-sleeve button-down. While downing a tall ice water, he watched through the back windows as the girls laughed and talked.

Jordan stood and started doing handstands on the beach. Clearly, an athlete. But his gaze kept returning to Sam. The wind barely tossed a hair on her head wrapped in that tight bun. So reserved, and captivating. He wondered what color her eyes were behind those oversized sunglasses.

He went outside to hang up his suit and towel.

The girls collected their things to head back inside.

He kept his stares discreet. Until Sam climbed the few steps up their patio, and glanced his way.

He smiled and waved.

She didn't smile back, but lifted her hand in a small wave. Then escaped into the house.

Jordan strolled over to his deck, and knocked on the wooden railing. "Permission to come aboard?"

He chuckled. "Granted."

When she climbed the stairs, he leaned against the railing.

"Since you're a local, do you have any recommendations for a great place for drinks and dinner?"

He raised his eyebrow. "Depends on your definition of great. Are you looking for laid back and casual, or something fancier?"

She smiled. "I think my friend needs something more relaxing."

"My buddy owns a place a few blocks over, the Breakwater Bar & Grill. Right up against the beach, open-air." He motioned with his head. "They have a live band all weekend for the Fourth."

Her grin widened. "Sounds perfect. Care to join us?"

He kept a smirk to himself. "I have other plans." He glanced over at the patio where Sam laid out their towels and her soaked cover-up. Trying to appear disinterested, but Chase caught her sideways peeks. It had been a long time since he'd seen anyone that interesting rent the place next door. Normally, snow birds and rich old men with too-young wives—or mistresses—occupied the house.

He'd be damn lucky to date a woman like Sam. "But maybe I'll run into you ladies."

"I hope so. See you around." Jordan left, and sauntered into their house.

I'm actually looking forward to my shift tonight.

SAM, HURRY UP!" Liddy called from the living room.

She clomped down the stairs in her beach sandals, capri pants, and gray, collared sleeveless shirt that buttoned up the front. The most casual-sexy outfit she'd packed.

Jordan looked over from her phone, and her eyes narrowed. "That is *not* casual-sexy."

Liddy buried her face in her hands. "How did we ever let it get this bad?"

"What's wrong with it?" Unlike her bikini, it fit Sam nicely, was comfortable, and revealed a bit of her shoulders. Kind of.

"Are those sandals or loafers? What cow died to make those?" Liddy pinched the bridge of her nose.

Jordan put down her phone, and gave her a sad smile. "Sam, I love you. It's time for an intervention."

"Excuse me?" She raised a perfectly manicured brow.

"It's come to the point where you don't know *how* to

relax. You can't even identify sexy anymore. And you're the sexiest one of all three of us."

Liddy nodded. "It's like she threw out the manual when Lance dumped her."

Heat flushed her face. "He did *not* dump me. That whole thing wasn't going anywhere."

"Because of those sandals, right?"

Sam glared at Liddy. Jordan snorted.

"I'm so disappointed we waited years to fix this." Jordan held onto Sam's shoulders. "Go upstairs, and change into the sluttiest thing you brought."

"Uh, no. That's not the kind of vibe I want to give off."

"I promise your version of slutty is nowhere near what real-slutty is."

Sam rolled her eyes on a sigh, and turned back to the stairs. "Fine. I'll just go grab one of my business suits, then." *That'll shut them up.*

"If you do, I'll rip it off, and shove you into a pair of my Daisy Dukes." Jordan crossed her arms.

She cringed inside. Those suckers hardly looked comfortable at all. If this was a vacation, she wanted to be *comfortable. That's the point of holidays, right?*

Jordan maneuvered past her on the stairs, and dashed into her room. "I'll find something myself. If you really don't have anything suitable, you can borrow one of my dresses. You *have* to look stellar. That Chase guy might be there."

Her stomach twisted. "You invited *him?*"

Jordan didn't answer, just rummaged through Sam's bag like a lioness mauling a gazelle. Then moved to the armoire, and fished through the hangers. She grinned, and pulled out a floral sundress. "This!"

Sam clenched her jaw and sucked in air between her teeth. That dress wasn't quite as old as her bikini, but definitely wouldn't fit either. She hadn't been thinking when she threw that thing in her bag, with so little time to pack. "That won't fit."

"Try it for me."

She pursed her lips. The last memory she had of that dress was a date night with Lance, who'd spent most of their evening talking on the phone for work. He'd hardly looked at her over dinner. Needless to say, that was the beginning of the end.

Now that she stopped to think, she didn't remember wearing a dress ever since. Just business suits.

Sam took off her clothes. It took the two of them to squeeze her into that thing, and tight didn't even begin to describe it. It was hard to breathe. When she looked down at herself, she wanted to die all over again. The lace in her bra peeked out above the bodice.

"You'll need a different bra," Jordan surveyed after she zipped her up. "Or better yet, go without."

"Are you nuts?"

"Trust me."

Sam complied, and wiggled out of her bra, tossing it on

the bed. Now, her breasts nearly spilled out over the top.

Jordan's jaw dropped. "*That's* the dress!" She covered her mouth. "Damn, woman. I knew your inner kitten was in there somewhere, and you're even sexier now than in college."

She wanted to dive under the covers. Fidgeting and trying to hide her cleavage didn't make her feel less vulnerable.

"I have the perfect strappy heels for this. You're still a size eight shoe, right?"

Sam sighed. "Jordan . . . " Her insecurity was off the charts.

Her friend stopped, and wrapped her in a hug. "You've buried yourself in work for too long. I'm just trying to help you have fun and be the Sam I know you are." She let go, and adjusted a curl by her ear. "Not all guys are shitheads like Lance. Not many women are true gems, like you."

She finally smiled, probably the first one of their trip, and hugged her friend back.

"Are you two finished?" Liddy called from the bottom step.

"Now, let's put on these heels," Jordan said. "And go get our drink on!"

Chapter FOUR

WHAT CAN I getcha?" Chase asked a couple standing at the bar of the Breakwater. He knew why David had called him to help out that night. The place was slammed with people—vacationers and locals alike. A profitable kick-off to the holiday weekend.

"A Corona and a screwdriver," they said.

Chase nodded and went to work mixing drinks. Every few minutes he'd glance up to see if Sam and her friends had arrived. *What's taking so long?*

String lights canopied the place with hanging paper lanterns featuring colorful hibiscus flowers. David had taken the luau theme to the extreme for the holiday. Honestly, Chase liked the atmosphere. Patrons had been dancing on the deck to the Caribbean steel drum band in the corner ever since they started to play a few hours before. The strong breeze blew the smoke from the tiki torches into the bar. Luckily, most everyone was too drunk or happy to notice.

Finally, the ladies strolled in the front entryway, all smiles . . . except Sam.

She scanned the room like a wary tigress, half annoyed, half bored, behind the rest of her friends.

She's gonna be a tough nut to crack.

But damn, if Chase wasn't up to the challenge. He'd seen her type before—wound tight because it gave her a sense of control.

Sizing people up was his specialty. His first impression was that she worked in corporate America. Lord knew he'd seen enough women trying to act like men to get ahead. That might explain why she went by Sam. She likely had a more feminine name, like Samantha, but refused to use it.

He looked up again from the beer he filled from the tap.

Fuck me!

Sam had maneuvered to Jordan's left, surveying the bar. She wore a white, spaghetti-strap dress with large raspberry-colored flowers printed on it that plunged at the neckline, and white strappy heels up her smooth ankles.

Chase's dick flexed in his shorts, and his mouth went dry.

"Chase!" David called from a few feet away.

He looked at his friend, the owner of the bar, who had his eyebrows up.

A cold slimy something ran down around his fingers. *Shit!* The glass had overflowed with beer, and Chase quickly slammed the tap back.

Christ! Focus.

The women found a table at the far side of the bar.

Chase wouldn't let this opportunity pass him by.

He delivered the beer after drying the outside of the glass. "Cover me," he called to David, and wend his way to the enticing vision.

As Roxie, one of the waitresses, approached to take their order, Chase gave her an all-clear.

"I've got this one."

Roxie raised a brow, but another patron called her over.

"Evening, ladies. Welcome to Breakwater. What can I start you off with?" He rested his hands on the backs of Sam and Jordan's chairs.

Sam stiffened, but tried to act casually by setting her small clutch on the tabletop.

Oh yay. Wound tightly means ready to explode.

"Your *other plans* meant bartending? Was this just a ploy to get more tips?" Jordan asked, beaming from ear to ear. "What's good here?"

"A screaming orgasm." Chase's standard response to any woman who asked such a blatant setup question.

Jordan and Liddy laughed. "We'll take three."

"No, I'll have a Manhattan," Sam corrected her friend.

Chase held back a grin when she jumped in her chair. A tell-tale sign that Sam got a kick to the shin under the table.

"Okay, I'll have a screaming orgasm," she said with a scowl.

Chase smiled. "Yes, you will. Only if you really want one, though." He winked before heading back to the bar.

As he fixed their drinks with lightning speed—making Sam's with a little extra care—the girls talked and snickered with each other. A dress never looked so enticing on a woman's body than Sam's. The urge to kiss along her exposed neckline, to stroke her bare skin, itched in his fingers. He finished off their drinks with a cherry garnish, and grinned to himself.

I'd love to taste her after she eats that cherry.

He carried them over, along with a few flowered leis. Most of the leis they handed out tonight were the fake plastic neon ones, but he made sure to grab the *real* flowers for this trio.

"Care to be leied tonight?" He set down the tray of drinks and carefully handed each woman her own lei.

Jordan and Liddy giggled, and Sam muttered, "Good grief." Taking the lei, she slipped it over her head.

He smoothed a finger over her shoulder, feeling the goosebumps rise. "Don't worry. It looks great on you." He returned to the bar to help some customers. He'd give her a few minutes with her drink to loosen up.

David reached over to grab a bottle of gin. "What's with city-girl?"

"Oh, her?" Chase motioned with his chin toward Sam. "That's the woman who'll be wearing my T-shirt to bed every night." *If she wears anything at all.*

SAM, LOOSEN UP. Try and have fun. Chase is just flirting with you," Jordan said.

Sam groaned to herself. Jordan was right, and the truth was Sam liked it. She liked the attention from this handsome, audacious surfer-boy. Which was just proof it had been way too long since she'd been with a man.

Crap!

Time for a distraction. She retrieved her phone from her purse, because she hadn't checked email since noon. Still no word from her boss on when the presentation would be. A passing waitress caught her eye. "Excuse me, miss. Do you have Wi-Fi here?"

Before the woman could respond, the phone was yanked from her hand.

"Hey," she screeched to Jordan.

"No phones." The stern tone in her voice was like nothing Sam had heard before.

Sam scowled.

Apparently, her response was not fast enough for Jordan's satisfaction, and she moved the phone over a full glass of ice water. And raised a reprimanding eyebrow.

She gasped. "You wouldn't."

"Are you willing to take that chance?"

Sam huffed. "Fine. I'll put the phone away."

Jordan handed her the phone, and she stuck it back in her purse, vowing to check later when she returned to her room. She glanced up briefly toward the bar.

Chase watched her with an amused, indulgent smile.

Her stomach did a little somersault, but she quickly looked away.

Damn! She reached for her drink, which wasn't half bad, and polished it off. About six more of those and she'd get a significant buzz, and forget about her poor laptop.

Before she could wallow much longer, Chase came to the table, holding a tray of drinks and a plate of appetizers. He set the drinks down and left the appetizers in the center of the round table.

"What's this?" Liddy asked, leaning forward.

"My treat." Again, he placed his right hand on the back of Sam's chair, skimming her shoulder in the process. "Jalapeño poppers, pineapple wrapped in bacon, coconut grilled shrimp, and Hawaiian pork sliders."

"Wow." Jordan's eyes rounded. "Looks great. And what's this?" she asked as she raised the cool glass to her lips.

"One of my specialties. Similar to a piña colada."

Jordan and Liddy both sipped. "Mmm. I love penis colossus." The girls laughed at Jordan's joke.

Chase chuckled. "You have one hell of a sense of humor." He looked at Sam. "And you barely cracked a smile. Having a rough day, Sam? I've got just the thing for that."

Sam glanced at Jordan, then Chase. "Look surfer-boy, you don't need to be wasting time flirting so hard. I'm sure you have other customers to help, or a board to wax or something."

Liddy threw her a glare across the table.

Sam was instantly ashamed. She hadn't meant the words to come across that harsh.

Chase's smile never wavered, in fact, it only grew. Then, he shocked the hell out of her. He leaned down and whispered in her ear, "Don't you ever let your hair down?"

Despite herself, shivers raced down her spine and curled her toes.

Speechless, she watched him stand tall, wink, and return to the bar.

She couldn't resist a glance at his muscular, round ass.

Oh, heavens above. The closer he got, the hornier she became. Please help me get through this night, she begged herself. *Please help me get through this vacation with him right next door.*

Jordan pushed her piña colada toward Sam. "Drink up, girl. You need it. Then, we're going over there to dance." She pointed to the steel-drum band.

Sam took the drink to her lips and tried a tentative sip. Sweet, refreshing, with an extra after-kick. *Hm, not bad.* She gulped a bit more, and reached for a pineapple munchie. *Crap! These are good, too.*

The girls snacked their fill and emptied their glasses.

After a few minutes, Jordan announced, "Let's go dance." Liddy popped up, and Jordan took Sam's hand.

"Okay, I'm coming."

"Not yet, you're not," Jordan said with a sly smile.

Liddy laughed along with Jordan, and Sam couldn't hold back. She let out a belly laugh and it felt so damn good. Jordan had a wicked smart sense of humor, and maybe that was one reason they'd been such good friends for so long.

Sam followed them to the side patio that served as the dance floor. The girls danced through several songs among the throng of people. Sam smoothed the hair from her face and tucked a few strays back into her bun. Perspiration lined her forehead, and more trickled between her breasts, but she didn't let that stop her. It wasn't that she didn't know how to have a good time, it just took a little longer to get into "vacation mode."

Occasionally, Sam glanced at the bar to watch Chase at work. Attentive, friendly, and he wasn't bad to look at. *They don't grow 'em like that in San Fran.*

Once or twice, she noticed him looking at her, and maybe the alcohol started kicking in because she didn't even let it bother her. In fact, her harsh words from earlier caught up with her guilt.

When the music switched to a slower beat, she caught his gaze again. And mouthed, *I'm sorry,* with a smile.

He grinned back, in the middle of shaking a martini for someone, and winked at her.

A young guy tapped her on the shoulder and asked for a dance. Maybe twenty-two, six feet tall, with bleach highlights and a coy smile, but not her style. Or age. She fanned herself, apologizing and using the heat as her excuse to deny him.

Finally, Liddy shouted. "Let's take a break. I need a drink."

"Agreed," Sam shouted back.

Maybe their very attentive surfer-boy would be available to take their drink orders. Sam was parched.

They arrived at the table, and fresh drinks were already waiting, along with a round of water. *How sweet.*

Sam dabbed her upper lip with her napkin and grabbed the glass. Mmm, another good choice. This one tasted like rum punch.

"Okay." Sam leaned closer to her friends. "My turn to play matchmaker."

Jordan's eyebrows rose. Liddy smiled.

"Alright."

Sam tapped her index finger on her chin as she scoped out the place. There were a handful of couples, but certainly enough selection for Sam to pick out for her single friends.

"Ah, how about him?" She pointed to a blond standing with a group of guys at the end of the bar. Just under six-feet, green eyes, in a Hawaiian shirt with the posture of a banker or lawyer.

Jordan's lips curled at the edges. "He could work. I'd need to see how long his fingers are though." She craned her neck to get a fuller view.

Sam swatted at her friend. "Get your mind out of the gutter."

Jordan wiggled her brows, and all three girls laughed.

"You do have a dirty mind," Liddy chimed in.

Chase arrived at their table. His hand rested on the back of Sam's chair, his thumb absently stroking her bare shoulder.

Tingles raced along her skin, and filled her with sensations she thought long gone.

He leaned forward to ask, "How are you ladies doing? Need another round?"

"Chase, these drinks are yummy. Keep 'em coming," Liddy said.

All three ladies laughed at their inside joke.

Chase grinned. "Okay. Will do." Then he bent to whisper in Sam's ear. "You're gorgeous when you laugh. Apology accepted."

Sam bit her lip and willed herself not to squirm. "Thank you," she muttered.

Frick! His delicious hot breath caressed her yet again. She wished to her core she didn't like it so much. How could a man have such an effect on her with a mere whisper? She ignored the heat gathering at the apex of her thighs.

After maybe an hour or two—she couldn't be sure—they ate a little, drank a lot, and danced, if one could call it that. Sam couldn't remember having so much fun. Several more men came up and started dancing with them, their hands liberal on her waist or hips, but nothing Jordan couldn't handle by shooing them away. By the last dance, Sam couldn't have cared less about the bystanders. Spending time with her girls was more fun than she'd had in years.

The trio somehow managed to stumble to their temporary home and their temporary beds. Dreams of tall, blond, and handsome surfers filled Sam's head causing her lips to curve into a sleepy, drunken smile.

Chapter
FIVE

CHASE CARRIED A tray of freshly brewed coffees up the ladies' back porch. From the number of drinks they pounded last night, he was sure all three of them had the grandmother of hangovers. He'd know. He'd made every one of their beverages.

He'd watched Sam down each concoction with genuine appreciation, and gradually, that ice wall around her chipped away. When she'd finally let her guard down and started having fun, she was glorious.

The sun rose several hours ago, and he hadn't heard a peep from their house yet. He approached the back sliding door slowly, not to scare them if they were already awake. After a firm knock, no one came down. Then another knock, and a head popped up from the living room couch.

Liddy. But she merely turned over.

Yeah, they're really hungover.

A shadow moved by the staircase, and Sam's adorable feet came into view. After another step, her knees. Then her glorious flowered sundress from the prior night, and finally her face.

He sucked in a breath.

Her hair was still wrapped in a bun from the night before, and her mascara was smudged. When she wiped the sleep from her eyes, more makeup smeared.

Her feet reached the bottom step, and he knocked lightly once again.

She looked up, and met his gaze.

He raised the tray of coffees, and smiled.

She smiled back. A small one, but genuine. After opening the sliding glass door, she winced at the extra sunlight. "You're an early riser, aren't you?"

For you, hell yes.

"You three could've taken a whole ship of sailors in a drinking contest."

Sam leaned forward and smelled the steam from the small openings in the lids. "That is divine. Are you a mind reader as well?"

"Yeah, coffee for the morning-after blitzers. Real genius I am. Do you need creamer?"

"We have some. Come in." She took the tray and carried them into the kitchen.

He followed at a safe distance, giving her space and watching her hips sway in her stroll. Liddy and Jordan sprawled on the couches with pillows and blankets over their heads. Interesting, they hadn't heard Chase knocking, but Sam heard from the second floor.

"How do you take yours?" Sam asked.

He opened his mouth to respond just sugar, but his mouth froze halfway open.

Sam rose on tiptoes, and reached up into the cabinet, revealing the side of her dress. Unzipped, all the way to the bottom of her ribcage, exposing the side of one extremely creamy breast.

His tongue swelled, and he couldn't think of words to respond. *What was the question?*

Her curves and that supple skin looked good enough to feast on. He couldn't tear his eyes away. The combination of messy hair, smeared makeup, and the sleepy morning-after look, she was fucking adorable. He loved that she never even made it out of her dress last night, which meant he was having a positive influence on her.

Her friends were having a positive influence on her, too.

The woman was finally enjoying her vacation.

And he was enjoying the view. Way too much. Once again, his dick wasn't behaving. He adjusted his shorts, thankful she faced the other way.

"Do you have to make so much noise?" Liddy's strangled voice called from the couch.

"Chase brought coffee," Sam answered. "Can't you smell heaven?"

"Surfer-boy has great taste," Jordan's muffled voice came from the couch. "But tell the gentleman it's way too early.”

A ping of guilt hit Chase's core. Perhaps he'd made them a few too many drinks last night.

“It's ten-thirty a.m., and thanks for the label.”

Sam glanced his way as she poured creamer, and a slight pink tinged her cheeks.

He guessed she was the one who created the nickname. Not that he minded, not even the juvenile implication. At least it meant she was thinking of him.

He walked over and helped pull the coffees out of the tray, and sprinkled some sugar into one. Then held it up. “Cheers.”

She chuckled, and tapped lids. Her mouth curved around the opening of the coffee, drinking in the heat and letting out a sigh.

He swallowed down a groan. How badly he wanted to be that coffee lid. No, more than that. Watching her with her guard down, nursing her hangover, and the always-present knot in her hair, he could think of only one thing. He wanted to fuck the conservative right out of her. He imagined lifting her skirt over her sexy ass and taking her over her desk in her office. He'd love nothing more than to show her life meant more than work.

She hummed her approval, and the vibration reached his skin. Which zoomed straight to his dick.

“Thanks, Chase.”

He cleared his throat, and guzzled some coffee.

That's the first time she's said my name.

He wanted to hear it more often from her lips. In a more . . . passionate way.

With a final smile, he gave her another wink. "You ladies have a fun day."

DAMN, THAT MAN was charming. Sam couldn't hold back her blush from the moment he'd knocked on the back patio, wearing that sexy smile. She swore his gaze never left hers once she'd opened the door.

Like he was studying her.

The last thing she'd expected was for him to deliver coffee. His thoughtfulness shook her guard, and she couldn't help but accept. Though, she shouldn't be surprised. His overly attentive behavior at the bar last night—from what she could remember—was as thoughtful and sweet as it was overbearing.

Maybe. Sam's brain was still a little fuzzy.

Perhaps not overbearing. Dammit, maybe it was pure interest.

She reached into the cabinet for a cup for water, to chase down ibuprofen, when a breeze blew in from the patio. Along her skin.

Skin that should be covered by her dress.

Sam glanced down. The side of her dress was open, the zipper pulled all the way down below her bra. Or what *should* have been her bra, only she didn't wear one last night.

She'd been so drunk when they came home, she couldn't even make it out of her dress. Far too much of her breast was revealed.

Chase had seen the whole thing.

"Jesus!" She dropped the tumbler, which bounced around the counter, while she grabbed her zipper to pull it up.

Which was pointless, the damage was done. He'd already seen everything.

Escaping upstairs to get dressed, she passed a mirror in the hallway, and witnessed the rest of her disheveled state. Smudged makeup halfway down her face, and her hair . . .

God, like Medusa's worst hangover.

Only, she couldn't crawl back into her cave of damnation.

After a quick shower and a change of clothes, she tied her damp hair back into a bun and returned downstairs.

Liddy and Jordan sat at the breakfast bar, nursing their coffees and splitting headaches.

Sam wrinkled her nose. "What's that smell?"

"It's called ocean water," Liddy responded. The two burst out laughing, and instantly winced, grabbing their heads.

Sam smirked, and sniffed again. They were right. Just the scent of the ocean and lingering personal mortification.

I'M RUNNING OUT for coconut water, girls," Sam called from the kitchen. "It will hydrate us, and replace the electrolytes. Need anything else?"

Groans carried in from the living room. "No, and could you please whisper?" Jordan asked from her perch on the sofa.

Sam grinned. "It was your idea to go out." With that, she retrieved the car keys hanging on the hook by the front door.

After a quick check on her phone—still no email from her boss—and a fifteen-minute drive, she found a grocery store. She grabbed the water, and a few side dishes to go with the hamburgers for lunch. A nice greasy burger sounded perfect.

On the way back to the house, Sam noticed an oversized sign by a development, with Chase's large face smiling back at her.

She tapped on the brakes, not sure if she was hallucinating.

He was surrounded by a bunch of kids, with a 'Coming Soon' label advertising a special needs center.

What's that about?

Sam arrived at the rental house to find Chase re-mulching a palm tree in his front yard.

The memory of her partial flashing this morning made her cheeks heat. She forced the embarrassment aside. They were both adults. The fact that he didn't mention it probably proved he was just as off guard as her. Or a gentleman.

Do those still exist?

Besides, she really wanted to know the story behind the sign.

She lifted the canvas bag of groceries, and walked over. As she approached, she could practically smell the testosterone in the air.

"What gives with the billboard down the road? Are you a modeling surfer?"

"You think I could be a model?" he asked with a grin. Dirt covered his arms up to his elbows, and sweat glistened on his forehead.

She should be annoyed, although she was becoming slightly addicted to his smile. She forced a look of irritation.

"No. That's my land. I'm funding that place," he confessed.

"Funding what?"

"Why are you so interested?"

She rested her hand on her hip. "Do you answer every

question with a question?"

He paused, holding a pile of mulch in his hands. *Large hands.* Almost as large as his grin. "We just put up that sign to get public opinion on our side. It's really going to be an adult toy store."

She smirked, but couldn't deny that was funny.

"Okay, seriously."

"Okay. Seriously, it's an ASD Living Community." He continued working, but kept his torso facing her.

"ASD?" she asked, mildly intrigued.

"Autism Spectrum Disorder."

"Wow." She nodded. *Maybe he isn't a complete social loafer after all.* "Is that a personal issue for you?"

His grin returned. "If you let me take you out, I'll tell you all about it."

Tempting, especially since she began to doubt whether he really had a double-digit IQ.

"We'll see. I need to get inside. Potato salad in the bag. See ya, surfer-boy."

"See ya, beautiful."

She spun on her heel and smiled. His compliments shouldn't flatter her, but what was wrong with a little flirtation?

YOU'VE BURNT THE burgers." Liddy scowled over Jordan's shoulder as she cooked the meat on the grill.

"No, I didn't. They're well-done."

"More like hockey pucks." Sam set the plates of potato salad and fruit on the patio table. "Please, tell me that wasn't all the beef we bought."

"No," she replied as she lifted one on her spatula. "This one here is okay."

Sam peered over Jordan's arm. The third burger she referenced wasn't quite as black as the other two. But still not acceptable by her standards.

"How many patties do we have left? We need to start over."

Jordan huffed, and switched off the burners. "Fine. Don't touch anything, and I'll fix this." She sprinted over, and knocked on Chase's back door.

Sam stared at the burned beef. Eat overcooked burgers, or face *him* again?

Before she had time to process her preference, Jordan returned with Chase in tow. Freshly showered from his morning yard work, and dressed in a pair of cargo shorts and a gray T-shirt, not to mention that delectable smile.

"Jordan tells me you need help with some meat."

Liddy snorted. Jordan giggled.

Sam met his smirk head on. "Jordan doesn't know how to handle prime beef."

That made his grin widen, and even brought a small blush to his cheeks. "What a shame. Mind if I . . . ?"

"Only if you agree to stay for lunch." Jordan gave Sam

a discreet smile.

"How can I refuse an invitation from three women in distress?"

Liddy presented him with a fresh package of hamburger meat. He took over the task with ease, handled the grill like a red-blooded American male for a bunch of burgers to erase their hangovers.

First coffee, then grilling. Pretty attentive for a surfer-boy.

Sam enjoyed the view—the ocean *and* the man. Sunshine chased away the morning clouds, and glittered off the water like sparklers. The way a beach was supposed to look, not foggy like in San Fran.

Lunch hit the spot perfectly, thanks to Chase. The grease absorbed the remnants of their hangovers, and his charm wiped away the remnants of her prejudices. Or most of them. It was hard to hold onto slanted impressions when he kept smiling at her and cracking up her friends.

"Crap! We're out of beer." Liddy frowned over the cooler.

"I have some more at my house." He gazed at Sam. "Care to join me?"

Sam held her breath. The invitation was tempting.

"Sure!" Jordan jumped up from her chair.

They followed him across the beach up to his back patio, and he invited them in through his sliding door.

When Sam stepped through, he glided his hand across

the small of her back. A casual gesture, with no real purpose behind it than showing her in and closing the door behind her, but her skin still tingled from his touch.

His house appeared more spacious than their rental, clearly intended more for comfort than for show. A slouchy chamois tan sofa with soft green pillows looked super cozy. He'd probably passed out on those a few times over the years. Or on the sage green frieze area rug. Comfy under her bare feet.

The room connected to the large kitchen behind a granite breakfast bar, and the darker tile floor—made to look like wood—contrasted nicely against the lighter walls. Green accents filled the house, along with framed photos. Two women around Chase's age smiled in the pictures, with his arms around their shoulders. Then a few more with whom she assumed were his parents.

"Damn, Bradshaw. You've got good taste." Jordan's gaze circled the room.

"I'll tell my sisters you said that. They did all the decorating."

"What's that?" Her brows pinched together as she pointed to the corner of the room by the sliding doors to a pegboard, covered with random items.

Faded photos, vintage keys, coil-shaped conch shells, a rusty clock, and even a dingy, white bikini top dangling from the edge.

Sam tilted her head. *Strange decor.*

He grinned. "That's my contribution. I find some weird things out in the ocean. These were good enough to make the wall."

She grabbed one of the strings on the bikini. "Including naked women?"

He chuckled. "I find more of those than you'd think."

"Why did this one earn a spot on the wall?"

His grin widened. "Turn it over."

The bikini mimicked an older style, from the forties or fifties, with a straight band and more-pointed cups. On the inside breast pocket, a word marred the fabric in faded ink. "Marilyn?"

He reached into his fridge, and pulled out a few beers. "Found that on the rocks a few years ago. Probably just a fan being silly, but the signature matches Marilyn Monroe."

She raised her eyebrows. "You're saying this is Marilyn Monroe's?"

He shrugged and opened the first bottle. "Maybe. But even if it's not, still a fun idea."

Jordan and Liddy came over to look for themselves. "Certainly a conversation piece," Jordan noted.

"Pick your poison, ladies." He opened another beer, and handed it to Sam. The same brand she drank earlier.

"Actually," Jordan strolled to the back door. "I need limes for this beer. How about you, Liddy?" She cast her a knowing smile toward the door.

Liddy looked confused at the beer in her hand. Then

her eyes widened. "Oh, yeah. Me, too. Thanks, Chase."

The two left through the back without giving Sam a chance to respond.

"I have limes here," he announced, but her friends were gone.

Nice ploy, ladies.

"Do you want a lime?"

"No, thanks." She studied a picture on the bar of him with two other women. They both had the same color hair as Chase, and the same cobalt eyes.

"My little sisters."

"I figured. Clearly, not so little anymore. How old?" Sam asked.

"Ava is twenty-six, and Reese is twenty. Ava and I pretty much raised Reese after our mother died."

"So, you're close?"

He nodded, and sipped his beer, his hungry gaze focused on her face.

"How long ago did that happen?"

"My mother? Twelve years ago. Breast cancer."

Sam frowned. "I'm sorry. How old were you?"

"Eighteen. Reese was eight, and knee-deep in her behavioral therapy program."

She tilted her head.

"She has ASD."

"Oh." *Should I say sorry again? Seems like the wrong thing to say.* "That's why you're building the center?"

He nodded, and came around the counter. He stood next to her, looking at the picture, their bodies only a few inches apart.

His cologne was subtle, clean and fresh.

Is it him, or is the beer getting to me?

"What are they doing now?" she asked, to distract herself from his expansive frame so close.

"Ava is a real estate agent in San Jose, and Reese is an app developer."

"Seriously?"

His smile turned proud. "She's ridiculously smart. Reese got the help she needed early enough in life, now she's self-sufficient."

"That's awesome."

"There are many others who aren't as fortunate, and nowhere near enough places to help."

The man grew more intimidating the longer she talked to him. Handsome, athletic, superior charm, and a bona fide do-gooder. Perhaps an activist.

Her chest warmed, and it was hard to draw a deep breath.

"What are you thinking?" he asked, his gaze playful.

"Nothing." She hid the lie behind a sip of her beer.

He leaned against the counter, pushing in closer to her. "I was serious earlier. Do you ever let your hair down?"

Forcing a breath into her lungs was much harder with him so close. She opened her mouth to answer, but stopped when he reached behind her head.

He leaned in.

Her heart raced.

With a gentle grip, he slowly pulled the two pins from her hair, one by one, and let her curls drop down her back. Then, he laced his fingers through the strands, and fluffed them around her shoulders.

He hummed his approval. "You smell like oranges."

"It's, um, my shampoo. Blood orange and passion fruit."

His eyes traveled down her hair draped over the front of her chest, stopping two inches above her nipple. He lifted a lock of her hair and brought it to his nose. "I like it," he said in low tone.

The air charged around them.

He glanced into her eyes before he took the beer bottle out of her hand and leaned back to set it on the bar. His hands then slowly slid up her arms to cup her jaw.

"I've wanted to do this since the moment I saw you on the beach."

"Wha—"

His lips feathered over hers, soft and hesitant. The heat from his breath filled her mouth on a tiny gasp.

God help her, she couldn't help herself. She pressed into him, giving him the permission to proceed, and herself the permission to let go. Finally.

What began slow at first, quickly gained momentum.

His tongue sought hers, testing and sliding timidly. Her hands gripped his as she leaned into him. He tilted her head and took the kiss deeper, demanding more.

His hard body against hers felt like heaven.

A hand glided down her back and cupped her ass.

She mewled and grasped her hands around his neck.

He lifted her thigh, bringing her closer into him, aligning her with his cock. Dear God, he was so hard.

He groaned before he pressed his kisses against her neck, licking and sucking along the way. *Oh, that mouth.*

She dropped her head back and panted for air, savoring his lips on her skin.

Listening to her rigorous breath, it hit her. She wasn't some wanton, unprincipled woman who slept with any man willing to show her attention.

She pushed back, lowered her leg, and stepped away. So they no longer touched.

Chase blinked. "What's wrong?"

What was she thinking? *I'm an idiot.*

She shook her head several times. "I have to go." She spun and headed for the back door. "I'm sorry. I have to go."

Chapter SEVEN

YEAH, I HEARD you the first time," Chase said to no one. Sam left out the back door, leaving him standing alone in his living room, and watching her scramble down his steps.

She's a pearl. A pearl in a clamshell that's glued *shut. Shit!*

Patience, Chase.

He was nothing if not patient. A smile curled the corners of his lips.

With Sam, he'd need slow, methodical steps. He rarely worked this hard for a woman. Hell, maybe never. But Sam was different. Not just her gorgeous body, but *because* of her gorgeous body. The way she straightened her back when she thought she was getting pushed around. The confidence in her gait. The delicate strength of her neck. Her precious desire to *not* look desirable for fear that others wouldn't take her seriously.

Add to the growing list, the way she kissed with her whole body.

He groaned.

He *had* to have her, and one glance down told him a cold shower or two lay in his immediate future.

SAM RUSHED THROUGH the backdoor of the rental house to find her friends loading up the cooler with drinks and snacks for the beach.

"Hey, look what we found in the laundry room," Liddy called as she lifted a collapsible beach chair.

Sunning in the sand or watching the sunset was the last thing on Sam's mind. Her thoughts raced as fast as her heart. "That's great. I'll catch you guys later. I need to check email."

She rushed up the stairs, and maybe heard Jordan say something like *she shut him down.*

Sam didn't give a rat's ass.

Splashing water on her face cooled the raging hormones a bit.

Rationalizing her behavior came down to only one conclusion. Her body was retaliating. Simple as that.

After years of dormancy, she finally had her mind distracted from work long enough to notice—and appreciate—a good-looking man.

All right, fine, a great-looking man. A demigod, even. Easy on the eyes, charming with a caring heart, and a *damn good* kisser.

Her lips still tingled from his tongue. Where he'd

branded himself on her. Her body was awake once again, finally.

Her phone received a dozen emails throughout the day, but she couldn't focus on reading, responding, and opening the damn attachments. She replayed the kiss with Chase over and over. And her reaction.

"I *ran* from a hot man wanting to make out with me," she muttered in disgust.

Chucking her phone back in her purse, she went to her toiletry kit, and re-twirled her hair on top of her head—using two new hairpins.

The man had pulled out her other pins, wanting to see her free and loose, and she'd bolted. As if she were afraid to see herself with her hair down.

Her reflection revealed how flustered she was. Sun-kissed cheeks melded with a permanent blush, and an uptight updo. "Story of my life."

Meticulous updos, pant suits, and minimal makeup were so important throughout her adult life, her career. How else did she expect people to take her seriously? Many in her line of work—men, specifically, who maintained a glass ceiling over her head at every turn—took blonde and busty for bimbo. She *refused* to be passed over for promotions and bigger commissions because of the stereotype.

But now, for the first time, she realized she may have swayed too far on the other end of the spectrum. When there was no work to do, vacation her only focus, she couldn't enjoy herself or her femininity.

"Oh, to hell with it," she told the image in the mirror. She yanked the pins out of her hair, letting it fall down her back. Then, she leaned into the shower and turned on the faucet at full-blast. She stripped out of her clothes and stepped under the hot water. A scalding cascade.

Chase was not as he first appeared, perhaps. But what was he?

Sam couldn't reconcile the initial impressions with this generous, caring man so determined to crack the shell she'd so precisely constructed.

Satisfied she'd washed away the morass of the day, she plodded out and toweled off. She slipped her short, cotton nightgown over her. After pulling her novel from her canvas bag, she crawled in between the covers. It may be earlier than her typical turndown, but she needed the quiet time.

She also needed to consider maybe ending her dry spell.

Chapter EIGHT

WAKE UP, SLEEPY head."

Sam jumped from lying in bed, dropping her novel on the floor. She'd fallen asleep with the book half open, again.

Jordan picked up the book, and grinned over her. "As much as I love that you're reading a romance novel—that author is awesome by the way—you need to get out of the house."

Sam groaned, and rolled away, pulling the pillow over her head. "Vacation means sleeping in."

"Not for us, honey girl." She yanked off the pillow, and swatted her ass with it. "We are booked on a boat tour for snorkeling and whale watching. Time to go."

"Let me guess . . . " She rolled back over and smirked at her way-too-energetic friend. "Snorkeling was Liddy's idea."

Jordan put her hand on her hip. "When was the last time you went snorkeling? Or even just swimming?"

Sam scratched her head, and rubbed the sleep from her eyes, hiding the fact that she honestly couldn't remember the last time she'd done either. Except when she was a little kid.

"You are exhausting."

Truly. Wasn't it a few hours ago that she'd drunk an entire bottle of wine? That was only day two of the vacation drink-fest.

"We'll go shopping afterward," she sung, as if dangling that little treat in front of a toddler.

"Next time, lead with that."

AFTER SEVERAL HOURS of boating, snorkeling, and whale spotting, including a stop at Seal Island to see the sea lions, they finished off with a splurge downtown of a late lunch and a new vacation wardrobe for Sam. Including a slightly less revealing bikini, one she could move in without fear of spilling out. No more business suits or too-tight clothes.

They barged into the rental home, each carrying several shopping bags.

Sam grinned as she set down her loot, carefully pulling out every item, just as infatuated with her selection as in the store. Sure, she'd spent more than she intended, but this was her first vacation in years. And even longer than the last time she'd shopped for something other than work attire.

Admittedly, she'd thought of Chase a few times while deciding which outfits to buy. Imagining what he'd do, or say, when he saw her in them. A little thrill had run through her when she thought about her delicious surfer-boy with his super-fine ass.

Not that she was getting addicted to him.

"We are going out tonight, ladies," Jordan announced as she pulled out a new azure dress. "We have to show off and live it up in style."

Liddy set her new espadrilles on the table. "How about seafood? Surely, there are spectacular lobster places around here."

"Let's ask Chase for a recommendation. He must know all the best restaurants."

Sam bit her lip, staring at the white dress she'd bought in the store. As much as she wanted to see him, she knew Jordan always took things a step too far. She'd probably try to invite him after he provided a suggestion.

Sam wasn't sure if she was ready for that level of attention. Not after their kiss.

"I'll take care of that. Just a quick online search, and we'll pick the best one." She pulled out her phone. Score one for feminine independence. I maintain control.

Jordan gave her a sympathetic smile.

Please don't say anything. Just leave it be.

Thankfully, her friend didn't say a word. Just carried her bags upstairs.

"Perfect. Make reservations for seven p.m.," Liddy called, bounding down the hall to her room.

As Sam searched online for the best seafood restaurant nearby, she paused, realizing she hadn't once thought about work or her destroyed laptop all day. In fact, she hadn't even looked at her phone all day, either. Not the slightest urge to survey the ridiculous amount of emails in her inbox.

On a deep sigh, she glanced out the side window, to Chase's house. The curtains on his patio blew in the breeze, but nothing moved from inside his house.

Out the back door, the waves eclipsed those from this morning. A sliver of a surfboard peaked between the swells, and she recognized Chase's blond hair, wading farther out.

She fought back a smile, watching him excel at what he clearly loved.

When was the last time I felt happy like that?

Free, abandoned, and completely at peace with himself.

There was no more attractive feature in a man. A reserved confidence, even when he thought no one was watching.

She grabbed her dress and her bags, and raced upstairs to glamify herself for a five-star meal.

I can be that happy, too. I'll prove it.

Chapter NINE

DIVINE FOOD COMA," Liddy sighed, as she tossed her purse on the kitchen table, and stumbled to the couch. When she plopped down, she kicked off her heels, and snuggled into the cushions.

"By far, the best stuffed lobster on the planet." Jordan collapsed on the other sofa. "Heroic little crust—*hiccup!*—crustaceans, your sacrifices were not in vain."

"More like bait suckers." Sam placed their leftovers in the fridge. She didn't trust the other two to carry theirs; they were three sheets to the wind before dessert. "But you're right. That place was stellar."

Jordan rolled over, and gave Sam a smile. "Superb recommendation, Sammie."

"You're welcome." She poured herself a glass of water. "Come drink some water, and take a few painkillers before you—"

Soft snores came from both her friends, Liddy into the cushions, and Jordan into a chenille blanket.

"—pass out." Sam sighed.

They'd downed three wine bottles at dinner, while Sam only had two glasses throughout.

The night's fresh and mild air complemented the full moon, casting an amazing luminosity across the beach. She opened the back patio door, and let the cool breeze caress her face.

The scent of the sea filled her sinuses. A perfect night for a stroll. She slipped off her shoes, and walked down the stairs.

The sugary sand massaged her toes out to the surf, each wave softly hugging the shoreline in a rhythmic melody. The absence of people on the beach made everything more peaceful. In the dim moonlight, a few dolphin fins emerged from the water in the distance. A sliver of deep orange from the sunset still lingered like a thumbnail poking up from the horizon. She stood for several moments, inhaling the fresh air, taking in nature's beauty.

Sam dared a glance at Chase's house, through her peripheral vision. All dark.

He's probably at Breakwater. What does he do for a living anyway? There was no way tending bar part-time could pay the bills on that glorious beach house.

Continuing her walk, the warm breeze blew between her legs, and furled her new dress up around her thighs. She loved the silky feeling on her skin.

The water's surface was smooth tonight. She reached down, grabbed a shell, and rubbed the wet sand off between her fingers.

Memories of her trips to the shore with her parents filled her mind. Her father could skip a shell across the water with five bounces. Her attempts never made more than two.

Sam chucked it across the water, and it sank on the first hit. A laugh bubbled up from her stomach. She tried again with another shell, and it skipped only once.

"Try turning the other way."

She jumped at the familiar voice.

Chase stood behind her in a loose ice-blue T-shirt, and the same pair of cargo shorts she'd come to associate with him. His hair ruffled in the wind, and he'd never looked more comfortable. More dashing. More enticing.

"You snuck up on me."

"I called your name." He smiled.

"Didn't hear it."

"Try it the other way. Like a frisbee." He took a step closer.

Her cheeks warmed. She picked up another shell, and tried it. Straight into the water.

He chuckled again. "Takes practice."

Her lips curled at the corners. "Hmm."

"What's your full name?"

The question surprised her, but she didn't let it show. "Samantha Callahan."

He nodded. "Samantha. I like it."

Her name passing over his lips sank into her core like

smooth, warm chocolate. Her mouth watered. *Better than dessert.*

He made no attempt to hide his perusal of her from head to toe. "Nice dress. Is it new?"

She nodded.

"Vacation agrees with you, Samantha," he said with a grin. "I see you're still having trouble letting your hair down."

She lifted her hand and stroked down the back of her hair. "I only clipped it back to keep it off my face."

WHEN CHASE HAD walked out to his back deck that night, he surmised from the absolute quiet that the girls had gone out to dinner. He had to grin when he heard them return. The whole street heard them, from their obvious inebriation. They'd raved about lobsters, and he'd chuckled.

Nearly finished with his favorite IPA, he watched Sam stroll onto the beach and absorb the final moments of another glorious sunset. Beach life at its best.

Sam hadn't seemed to notice him, but damn, he noticed her. That white dress she wore looked soft and feminine. It hung loosely, but also showed off her curves. The back had some kind of wide-lace crochet straps that crossed over smooth, sun-kissed skin.

Damn!

He stepped closer, subtly shaking his head. "Uh-uh. All

the way down. Let me try."

Chase knew to tread lightly. The way she'd raced from his house the prior day rang in his head.

From his experience, women who let themselves get so tightly wound—feeling responsible for everything and needing control—struggled with trusting a man to take charge, and at least for a moment, take the helm. But this wasn't about control, or claiming. This was about showing her life was worth enjoying. Taking pleasure in each other's willingness.

Her eyes widened. After a beat, she raised her chin, and met his stare, an irresistible dare in her sparkling blue eyes. "Okay, you do it."

He held back his smile, thrilled by the challenge. He moved closer—close enough to smell her light floral fragrance. He reached behind her head, and found two pins, pulling them gently. Her hair tumbled down her back, and unfurled over her shoulders.

"There you are. Nice to meet you, Samantha."

He moved closer, caressing his fingers through her long silky hair, massaging her scalp.

Her eyelids fluttered, as if resisting closing entirely.

"Your hair is beautiful. Close your eyes. I won't hurt you."

She trusted his words, and complied.

His fingers caressed her skin, continuing his ministrations through her hair, when her head rested back into his hands. He bent down close to her ear and whispered, "You look even more beautiful when relaxed."

She sighed.

He gently kissed the sweet spot just beneath her ear.

Her breath hitched, but she didn't pull away.

He placed another kiss farther down her neck, and again.

Her head dropped to the side, giving him access, and his cock swelled in his shorts.

She smelled delicious.

He slid his hands down, landing one on her lower back, the other cupped her neck. His kisses traveled slowly to her soft, full lips, giving her time to protest.

She didn't.

In fact, when his lips landed on hers, she opened for him . . . her tongue waiting. The kiss grew to something more urgent, more primal and hungry. White wine lingered in her mouth, a crisp Riesling with a sweet aftertaste. He swallowed her moan, and demanded more.

Her arms wrapped around his neck and her body pulled into his.

Unadulterated lust surged through his body.

"Chase," she breathed.

He broke the precious contact at their lips to glance around. Even though the beach was empty and no one appeared to be watching, they still needed more privacy. Somewhere close; he couldn't risk breaking their sultry spell.

Spotting a grouping of palm trees set amongst tall, prairie grass at a neighbor's several doors down, he grasped Samantha's hand and led her away from the open, sandy area. The other rental house on the street was completely dark, and the owners lived in Canada, so he had little concern about spectators.

He leaned her against a palm tree and cupped her face in his hands. "I could kiss you all night, Samantha."

He glanced one last time at her irresistible lips, a mouth that pleaded for him to kiss her. He bonded his lips to hers without waiting another moment.

Her arms swung around his neck, molding her body to his. Her nipples poked through her thin white dress, nudging against his chest.

Fuck!

His breathing was like hers—heavy and needy. He wanted her right then, more than he could recall wanting another woman.

"Samantha," he breathed against her lips.

He slid his hands to the sides of her breasts and gently brushed his thumbs over her nipples.

Her head dropped to the side as she moaned.

On the quietest of breezes, Chase caught the scent of her arousal.

His raging erection nearly exploded in his shorts. *Fuck!* What he could do to her.

His next move had to be tactful and cautious.

He dropped his right hand to her hip and slowly caressed her, squeezing her beautifully rounded ass. He returned his lips to her warm, soft neck, and as his hand slid to her bare thigh, he begged. "Let me touch you. Let me make you feel good."

She mewled her response, and he didn't hesitate one nano-second.

Traveling under her light dress, his hand swept over her warm soft skin, to the lace of her thong. He teased and tempted, gently stroking his fingertips over her dew-wet sex.

He had to show her what she could feel when she let go. More importantly, she had to be the one to know she could get there, and there was no shame in giving in to the pleasure. Resigning control sometimes could be a very freeing thing.

His fingers persisted over the lace as his lips devoured her neck.

"Chase, please, more."

Finally. The words he fucking ached to hear.

He slipped two fingers under her waistband, slowly grazing over her lips before dragging a finger through her wet slit.

She moaned. Her nails dug into his scalp, gently pulling on his hair.

She was beyond ready.

He pushed a finger inside her, then two, going deep before retracting so very slowly.

Her head fell forward, resting against him. Her ragged breath warmed his neck.

He spread the wetness over her clit. As he pushed back inside her, she widened her stance. She was close, and he was more than eager to tip her over.

With two fingers inside her, he circled his thumb over her clit.

She gasped. Her body rocked into his hand to the same rhythm as the waves crashing on shore.

He increased the pressure and her muscles gripped his fingers. Her hands tugged on his hair sending tingles down his spine, straight to his dick. The rocking rhythm increased, her nipples so hard the peaks pressed against her dress.

Before she cried out, he crashed his lips over hers, taking in all the passion she finally released.

As her tremors subsided, he pulled out and smoothed her panties back in place.

She lifted her head to meet his gaze. "God, Chase, that . . . had to be the most intense . . . " Her words trailed off as she bit her lip and closed her eyes.

He smiled. The flush in her cheeks made her look so fucking sexy, but he couldn't take this any further right now. This was a giant step for her, and he didn't want to push his luck. "That's just a taste, darling. You are so incredible. How about we call it a night? Fireworks tomorrow and all that."

The corners of her kiss-swollen lips curved, and she nodded.

He took her hand, and weaving his fingers between hers, he walked her to her back door.

When they arrived, he cupped her face with his hands, leaned down and gave her a long—deep—goodnight kiss.

"Remember what I said about fireworks tomorrow, Samantha."

She nodded, and after a beat, her eyes lit up in understanding.

He pecked one last kiss on her mouth and retreated back to his house. "Goodnight."

"Goodnight, Chase," she whispered.

How in the world am I going to sleep tonight, knowing that delectable woman is sleeping only yards away?

Chapter
TEN

SAM'S CHEEKS HEATED the second she woke. Even hours later, the memory of that orgasm against the tree made her hot. She'd not had sex in nearly two years, and *that's what I've been missing?*

After a deep breath, she hobbled to the bathroom for a semi-cold shower. Chase had filled her dreams all night, and they were just as steamy as on the beach.

"If he could accomplish *that* with just his hands," she muttered to her reflection in the glass stall, "what could other parts of his anatomy accomplish?"

She towel-dried off, and braided her wet hair back, then put on her black lace shorts and lime green tank top, an outfit she'd bought yesterday for the beach.

In the living room, Jordan and Liddy replayed the same hangover show as the other morning. Sam chuckled, and fixed a cup of coffee, then made breakfast for her suffering friends. Greasy bacon, buttered toast, and eggs to soak up all the booze.

"I'll forgive you for making all that noise," Jordan piped

up from the couch, "because it smells really good in there."

Sunshine beamed in through the back patio, the waves just as gleaming as last night, and the ocean a breathtaking blue. Sam opened the door to let in a fresh breeze. The same sea-salt air from the night before, reminding her of that incredible climax . . . from Chase's expert fingers.

"Happy Independence Day," she sighed into the wind. Then she fixed a plate of food for herself.

"You're extra chipper this morning." Jordan eyed her as she plopped into a chair at the breakfast bar.

Sam set down a loaded plate and hot coffee in front of her. "Helps that I didn't down a case of wine in one sitting."

Jordan tipped her head. "No, you're actually glowing."

"That's what vacations do. Speaking of which, I let you both sleep in, unlike you did for me during my hangover."

Liddy sat beside her, cradling her head. "Aspirin. For the love of God, aspirin."

Sam poured her a glass of water, and set the bottle of pills in front of her, like a doting mother.

Liddy looked at her sideways. "What's up with you?"

"I know, right?" Jordan sipped her coffee, eyeing her over the rim. "It's like she got laid or something."

Sam pressed her lips together, and hid her blush behind a bite of bacon.

Jordan and Liddy's eyes widened at the same time. "Did you?" they asked.

"Of course not."

Jordan's eyes narrowed. "What did you do after we came home last night?"

"It was still early. I went for a walk on the beach."

"Who was with you?" Liddy asked in a melodic voice.

A knock pounded on their patio doorway. "Mornin', ladies."

Sam's gaze met Chase's gorgeous face across the room.

"You all look like you had fun last night," he chimed.

Damn, that smile did crazy things to her stomach.

"Yeah, in the future, remind me to stop after the second bottle." Liddy downed the rest of her water.

Chase chuckled, and leaned against the doorjamb. The more he looked at her, the more Sam's body reacted to him. Remembered and ached for a replay.

"I came to invite you all to my friend's party this afternoon. He's taking his boat out into the bay, lots of food and beer . . . and finishing off with fireworks at night." He winked at Sam.

Her cheeks heated again. *Hell yes.* "Sounds like fun. What can we bring?"

Jordan and Liddy's heads snapped around at her, slack-jawed.

Chase's grin widened. "Suits, and towels. And your pretty selves."

"Sounds great. We'll be there," Sam replied.

"Everyone's gathering at the yacht club at two. See you then." Then he gave Sam one last smile before spinning around and heading back to his place.

"Who are you, and where did you take our best friend?" Liddy asked Sam.

"Cuz I'll send her a farewell email," Jordan added. "Informing her she's been pink-slipped, and replaced by fun-Sam."

She ignored their comments, and just grabbed her cup to top-off her coffee. Perhaps, her mind was opening up to *all* the possibilities of this vacation. Having had a taste of that man's skills, she was ready for the full buffet. After all, he'd promised *fireworks* . . .

AFTER FIGHTING THROUGH holiday traffic, Sam and the girls found their way to Santa Cruz's harbor, coolers in hand. Sam wore her new bikini under her lace shorts and tank top, leaving her hair back in the braid from this morning.

At the foot of the gangplank, Chase talked with a few of his friends, clearly waiting for her. She could tell, from his unabashed smile when he spotted them.

"Holy crap," Liddy laughed. "You've got some seriously loaded friends, Chase."

Which is when Sam registered the boat behind him. More specifically, the yacht.

At least three decks high and a hundred feet long, a gleaming white marvel decorated with American flags, streamers, and even an Uncle Sam piñata tied to the front, with at least ten people on the bow, and another six on the back.

When she reached Chase's side, he gave her a long kiss on the cheek, lingering by her ear. "Happy Fourth of July. Glad you made it."

"Happy Fourth, surfer-boy. Me, too."

Jordan and Liddy climbed aboard, chatting away with a few guests already.

"What does your friend do to afford this?" Sam asked.

Chase placed his hand on the small of her back and led her aboard. "Marshall used to work with me, back in the day."

She stopped once she reached the deck, holding onto the railing, and eyed him. "What did *you* used to do? Drug running?"

He laughed. "Do I look like a mule to you?"

"Clearly, something lucrative."

"But not nearly as exciting, I'd imagine. Commercial real estate and development. Marshall scoped out new deals and opportunities, I closed them."

"Then what? Housing market crash?"

He laughed again. "Early retirement. At least for me."

She raised an eyebrow at him.

He tucked a stray hair behind her ear. "I like this look on you, Samantha. Braids are sexy. And useful."

"I hope so," she whispered.

He showed her around the yacht, introducing her to a few friends, and finishing off with getting her a drink. They both relaxed on the lounge cushions on the sky deck, soaking in the sun. A short while later, they pulled out of the harbor and into the bay. Music blared over the speakers throughout the yacht.

A tall, dark-haired man climbed the stairs, his eyes hidden behind aviator sunglasses. "Chase, my man. Glad you found some privacy on this hunk of junk."

"Stop gloating." Chase shook his hand. "Marshall Owen, meet Samantha Callahan, from San Fran."

Marshall shook her hand. "How do you know this old, retired geezer?"

"My girlfriends and I are renting the house next door for the week. Thanks for the invite. This is an impressive boat."

"Thank you."

"There you are, Marshall." A lady in a red dress climbed up the stairs, holding onto her blue sunhat in the wind. "So, this is where you've been hiding."

"From you, Claire? Never." Marshall walked over and kissed her on the cheek.

"Chase! So good to see you!" She leaned over and kissed him on the cheek, too. "Glad you could come."

"Thanks. Samantha Callahan, meet Claire Lonnigan. The best real estate agent this side of Palo Alto."

She batted the compliment away with her hand, but her

smile conveyed her appreciation. "Hi, Samantha." Then she turned back to her boyfriend. "What do you think of my new dress? Just for the Fourth."

"Looks phenomenal," Marshall answered. "Red is becoming on you." He wrapped his arms around Claire's waist, who giggled. "We'll bust out the champagne during the fireworks. Enjoy yourselves, you two." He and Claire retreated downstairs again.

Red is becoming on you.

Sam grinned at her reflection in the mirror. The new black skirt and red silk blouse she'd purchased just for her interview made her feel more confident. The perfect look for the start of a new career, and the promise of something more fulfilling. Higher up.

She paraded into the living room. "What do you think?"

Lance looked up from his smartphone, and grinned. "Damn. Is that for me?"

She scoffed. "For my interview tomorrow, silly."

"I'd hire you as my sexy admin, and take advantage of you in that skirt every damn day." He set down his phone, and spread his legs, inviting her to sit on his lap.

"I really need to make a good impression. This is my chance to move up."

Lance lost his smile. "Wait, are you serious?"

"Yeah."

"You can't wear that in an interview."

She looked down at her black heels. "Why not?"

Then he laughed. Actually, laughed at her. "There's no way they'd take you seriously dressed like that."

Her stomach tightened. "Dressed like what?"

"Red is too forward. They'll think you're a bimbo, and not a serious person." He gave her a sympathetic look. "You're not going to wear your hair like that, either, are you?"

She instinctively brushed back her blonde curls, which took two hours to fix. "What do you mean?"

He stood from the couch with a sigh. "You need to wear your hair back. Up in a bun or something." He took her hands in his, his expression almost pitying. "You need to aim for serious and reserved, not trashy."

Chase draped his arm around her shoulder, his gaze hot and focused. "I'm going to ask you a question, and I want you to be brutally honest with me."

Her mind reeled from the memory, all those years ago, but suddenly so fresh. "Okay," she stammered.

"Is that drink better than the ones I made for you at Breakwater?"

She smirked, and took another sip, licking her lips as she finished it off. "Nope."

"Good answer." He leaned in, pressing his lips against hers. "So sweet. Like that cherry garnish."

"Guys, you've got to check out this spread." Jordan and Liddy approached, carrying plates loaded with food. Both wore exuberant smiles.

Sam smiled at her friends. "Okay, lead the way."

Arriving at the buffet table, or more appropriately tables, Sam's jaw dropped. "Wow," she breathed.

"Good, huh?" Chase handed her a plate.

She couldn't decide where to start—shrimp, chicken, pork tenderloin, or crab cakes. She started with a bit of salad, then some kind of veggie-pasta dish and an oversized crab cake.

"I love that you don't just pick rabbit food," Chase whispered close to her ear.

Her heart pitter-pattered in a strange way when he said *love*, but she dared not examine something so superfluous. She grinned at him. "Oh, no. Food and I go way back. Is it always like this?" she asked as she motioned with her chin to the fare before them.

"You bet. Marshall knows how to throw a party. I have a few friends here. I'll introduce you later. We all take turns hosting parties, depending on the holiday."

"Hm. Which holiday is yours?"

"Super Bowl."

Sam laughed, and focused on her food. Conversations like this felt very boyfriend-girlfriend, and well, she couldn't think that far ahead.

Over the following few hours, people ate and drank, no

one really registering Marshall had piloted the boat half a mile out to the bay. He dropped anchor, still a safe distance from other boats, and joined his guests and Claire for the festivities.

The sun set, and the alcohol flowed freely. Jordan and Liddy danced to music pounding through the speakers. The lights twinkled brilliantly against the dark sky. The atmosphere was electric and exciting, the likes of which Sam hadn't experienced in some time.

"Dance with me." Chase stood, maneuvering in front of her with his hand outstretched.

She smiled and placed her rum punch on the ledge behind her.

His hand grasped hers and tugged her upright. He led her to an open space on deck, keeping her close, then wrapped his arm around her.

His body against hers fit like a dream. She'd never danced with a man like this before.

He wedged a thigh between her legs, drawing her in where they didn't have an inch of air between them. Damn! He felt so fine holding her—his muscles flexing with the music as they moved together.

Maybe it was the multiple rum punches, but tingles and a heat unassociated with the weather flooded Sam's body, dancing so incredibly close to Chase.

Her breath quickened. Letting herself go with the feeling, she suckled and kissed his neck. The growl from deep inside him reverberated through her lips.

"Samantha, you do things to me . . . I could take you right here."

She whimpered at the thought.

The crowd simply faded away.

He lifted her chin. Tipping his head, his lips claimed hers. Tasting her mouth, and sucking on her tongue. The kiss blossomed as she tilted her face, her tongue dancing with his.

With her arms snaked around his neck, she lifted to her tippy-toes. She desperately wanted to get closer.

Bam! Crack! Boom!

Sam jumped back and let out a small yelp. It took only a millisecond to notice the fireworks off shore.

Chase chuckled lightly. "Are you okay?"

"Yes. Just a little startled." Her heart already hammered in her chest, now for another reason.

"Me too," he said low in her ear. "First time I've kissed someone and literal fireworks go off. Been waiting my whole life for that."

His deep blue eyes practically glowed with passion.

The wet ache converged at the apex of her thighs. How she so wanted Chase to put an end to the hunger.

Out on the bay, with dozens of people around, there was nothing they could do. The ache would have to endure. They watched the fireworks, and everyone ahed and cheered. After a few minutes, the inferno inside cooled, and Sam enjoyed the show too.

Chase's attention never waned. Occasionally, he brushed his fingers on her skin, whispered in her ear, and held her hand.

The internal fire reset to low, and simmered for hours. It was all Sam could do to hold her patience. She craved the time alone with Chase, and his every touch only made her anticipate their post-fireworks playtime.

Alone and naked.

Chapter ELEVEN

THE PARTY ON the bay continued for another hour after the fireworks finished, and Chase thought it would never end. Waiting for Samantha to join him on the boat had been a true test of patience. Once he saw her smiling face, a calming pleasure had washed over him, the likes of which he'd never experienced before. However, like some horny teenager, within thirty minutes, he wanted her beautifully naked body in his bed. Underneath him, or on top and in control, didn't matter.

What started as a challenge to crack the ironclad barricade Samantha had built around her, quickly turned into something real. Something deep. Chase wouldn't deny it any more than he'd deny milk to a kitten.

As God as his witness, his feelings for Samantha also scared the shit out of him. How much time did it take to create that kind of connection? How much time would she need to come to the same conclusions? That they had something stronger than a vacation fling?

The moment the yacht docked, he leaned close to her

ear. "Let's go."

She glanced up at him. That knowing sparkle in her eyes shot electricity up his spine.

She wended through the crowd to Jordan and Liddy. Both women glanced his way, then Jordan whispered something in Samantha's ear causing them all to smile. After quick hugs all around, they said their goodbyes to his friends, and praised Marshall for another epic "boat party." Marshall never referred to his toy as a "yacht." He'd say, *Makes me old and stodgy.*

"Glad you could make it. And so great to meet you, Samantha." Marshall and Claire hugged her, and they were free at last.

In the car, Samantha only smiled. Chase couldn't tell if it was nervousness or anticipation.

"Did you have fun?"

She glanced his way. "I did. Thanks for inviting us. Your friends are really nice."

"They're great. I'm fortunate, like you, to have people I can count on."

Again, she merely smiled.

He reached for her hand. "Are you nervous? We don't have to do anything you don't want to." Although he'd give his left arm to have her say she wanted nothing more than to get naked with him.

"I'm not nervous at all."

"You're smiling a lot. Too many drinks?"

She shook her head, and stray hairs from her braid brushed her cheeks. "Do you really want to know?"

He grinned. "Yes, I do."

She smoothed her lips together and a delicate flush filled her cheeks. "I've been thinking . . . " She glanced over at him like a tigress hunting a meal. "I never gave head to a man while he was driving."

Chase's breath hitched. The car veered across the yellow center line. He straightened the steering wheel, and corrected the car. Thank goodness for no oncoming traffic.

He never imagined she'd say something like that.

He swallowed hard. His dick received that as an invitation. "Is this a fantasy of yours?"

She gave a sweet smile that Chase hadn't seen on her before. This woman was multifaceted, and fuck, if he couldn't wait to learn them all.

"I guess it is." Turning her body to face his, she asked, "Mind if I try?"

His dick was absolutely on-board. Ready and willing.

"You may," he managed to choke out.

She smiled and eased out of her seatbelt. Her hands quickly found his zipper.

He shifted his weight as she shimmied the fabric out of way.

With one delicate hand beneath his underwear waistband, she grabbed a hold of his cock. Using her free hand, she pushed down the cotton fabric, finally freeing his stone-hard dick.

She pumped a few times, and said, "You have a magnificent cock, Chase."

This woman was full of surprises. He didn't know she would even use that word.

"Thank you."

She lowered her mouth and wrapped her lips around his head.

"Fuck," he breathed.

Her tongue joined in, sliding through his slit, then down his length.

Chase backed off his speed a bit. Better play this safe; there was no rush.

Her mouth and hand worked in concert, sliding down and sucking on the way up.

Shit! At this rate, he'd explode in five seconds flat.

He cupped the nape of her neck, savoring any and all contact with her. *And that heat!* Her mouth was amazing. At a red light, he couldn't help himself. He gently held her head in place as he pumped twice into her mouth.

"Mmm." Her hum reverberated through his dick and up his spine. "See how long you can keep going." She resumed the glorious torture.

"Samantha," he panted. He was so fucking close, she might not appreciate cum all over her. She was too good at this, and holding back was nearly impossible. "Samantha," he repeated.

But the little wench heard him. She gripped hard, and sucked harder.

"Fuck," stretched from his mouth. His sac tightened, and heat flushed his face.

Barely making it into the driveway, he slammed the car into park, and growled out her name as she milked from him one of the best orgasms of his life.

His head collapsed against the headrest, breathing heavily. Damn-near passing out from lack of blood flow.

She lifted her head and righted most of his clothing.

He grabbed her hand and brought it to his lips, kissing once.

"How do you feel?" she whispered.

"You have to ask?" He met her gaze. "That was fucking awesome. Thank you."

She grinned. "You're welcome, surfer-boy."

He pulled up his shorts enough to cover himself. "Inside. It's your turn."

SHE ABSOLUTELY LOVED the gravel in his voice as he commanded her. Samantha was on a high from giving him a blowjob—she didn't know it could feel so good. And frankly, she was wet. Her panties were damp, and her sex pulsing.

She followed Chase into his dimly lit house. With no warning, he slammed the door shut and pinned her against it with his lips on hers.

His hands cupped her jaw and caressed her neck as the hunger in his kiss grew.

She swung her arms around his torso and let herself be consumed by him. By his passion. His desperation.

Her heart thundered.

He tunneled his hands between their bodies, breaking the kiss only long enough to whip her top over her head. Without ceremony, he unclasped her bra and sent it flying.

He stepped back, out of reach, taking her in. His eyes darkened with lust.

Sam basked in his approval.

"Take down your hair, Samantha." The words held a tone of request. She knew everything she did was her choice.

She unwound the hair tie holding her braid in place, then finger-combed some of the braid loose.

"More. All of it down."

She briefly pinched her brows together, then lifted her arms, and weaving her fingers at her scalp, briskly ruffled her hair loose.

"Perfect. Hold it right there."

Sam swallowed. She stood before him, naked from the waist up, with her hands at the top of her head.

His right hand caressed her blonde locks, pulling them forward. Repeating that several times, he watched them fall over her breasts. The back of his hand smoothed over her breast to her nipple.

She inhaled.

With both hands, he toyed with her nipples, seemingly fascinated by their response . . . peaked and as hard as diamonds.

Then he leaned forward and captured one in his mouth.

She gasped. His warm mouth felt divine, sucking and lapping at her.

He straightened, and stripped off her shorts and panties. She lowered her hands to help, and he stopped.

"Uh-uh. Just enjoy."

All right. She lifted her hands back over her head.

He continued, and she stepped out of her garments, shoes, too.

He stepped back again to savor her. His voice turned rough with desire. "Samantha, you are a goddess."

With him, she felt like one. God, no man had ever made her feel so sexy, so wanted before.

Touch me. Please touch me. Her body hungered for him.

He moved closer, his body heat spreading over her like a blanket. His hands slid over her hips, up the sides of her torso, cupping and fondling her breasts.

"Spread your legs, sweet Samantha."

She eagerly complied.

His lips lowered over hers, nibbling and gently sucking as his right hand glossed down her front, between her legs. When a single finger dragged through her slit, she moaned.

"So wet," he whispered over her lips.

His finger trailed the slickness to her clit, and circled.

More. She needed more.

As if hearing her words, he slid two fingers inside and pumped.

"Oh. God, Chase."

He grabbed her hands and lifted them higher against the door. Holding them against the wood with one hand, he used his other to dive into her farther with his fingers.

"Ah," she called out. She might come just like this.

But before she had a chance, he pulled his fingers out. Wordlessly, he took her hand off the door, and guided her to his bedroom.

As they walked in, Sam barely registered the slate gray walls, and the navy bedspread over a platform bed. Chase yanked off his shirt, spun her around, and pulled her flush against his body for a deep kiss with his talented mouth.

"I'm going to taste you, sweetness. You'll come on my tongue."

He backed her up to the bed, and she laid back. He released his shorts and let everything fall to the floor. He stood gloriously naked in the moonlight—broad shoulders, muscular abs, and an impressive length.

She practically drooled.

He grabbed a condom from the nightstand, rolled it on, and bent down between her legs. Smoothing a finger up her center, he said, "Look how plump you are."

Her fingers bunched his bed covers, smooth under her

touch.

Without wasting another moment, he dove his tongue right to her core.

"Ah," she panted.

His tongue worked magic on her needy clit. His fingers pushed inside, stroking her, driving her to the height of madness.

Her breathing came harder. Without much more effort, he tipped her over the edge into a wonderful abyss.

She cried out his name.

He didn't let up until she squeezed her legs around his head, her body out of control.

He climbed over her and inched her to the center of the bed. He lowered himself to his forearms and cradled her head, while the tip of his cock nudged her opening.

"I've thought about this moment since I saw you on the beach. You smiled at the ocean when you thought no one was looking."

Her eyes widened. She didn't even realize she'd done that. Before she could give it any more thought, Chase pushed smoothly—deeply—into her.

Her back bowed off the bed.

He kissed her neck—hot, open-mouthed—and stole her breath.

She wrapped her arms and legs around him as he thrust deeper, faster. The friction was deliciously raw, and it didn't take long for another quickening.

"Samantha . . ." he pleaded.

Her climax exploded mere moments before his. The whole room buzzed over her head from the intense rush.

He called out her name again—her full name—the sweetest sound to her ears.

By the time the ceiling stopped spinning overhead, she managed to drag her fingernails over his scalp. As if she could make him as tingly as her entire body.

His body shuddered. "That was so much better than I imagined." He dropped hot and breathy kisses along her neck to her cheek, and a final one on her lips.

She squeezed her legs around his ass, and massaged his calves with her feet. Every muscle smarted, and she smiled. "I'm too tired to move."

"Then don't." He pulled out and dispensed of the condom. He returned with a wet cloth to clean her, her body jerking with the soft and gentle touch.

Brought a blanket over them, he pulled her close.

The heat of their bodies and gentle rise and fall of his chest lulled her into a wonderfully deep sleep.

Chapter TWELVE

SHH," SAM BREATHED out through her teeth.

With two hands, she slowly, carefully opened Chase's sliding door, then reached down for her shoes. As she crossed the threshold onto his back deck, she made one last glance toward the stairs.

No sign of Chase.

Gently closing the door behind her, she exhaled a breath of relief. At four in the morning, she didn't want to wake him.

She scampered to her rental house, and climbed the stairs to her bedroom without so much as a creak on the floors. Then, when she stared at her reflection in the bathroom mirror, her hair all tangled, good and loved, that undeniable ping of regret hit.

She shouldn't have left him.

"Coward," she whispered to herself.

No, she had to leave. Getting attached to surfer-boy, when it was all about vacation sex, was a bad idea. Vacation sex meant live for the moment, no attachments.

Surely, even Chase understood that. By leaving, she avoided that awkward morning-after thing. Not that she had any experience with that. All her previous sexual escapades had been with boyfriends, so staying over was a given.

This was not a relationship.

But shit, was last night fun.

She'd swear it was like a first time. Like she'd never had sex before. Chase made her feel so alive. So incredibly alive. Something her girlfriends had wanted for her from the first day out here. Something she'd doubted she'd ever feel again. Yet, here she stood, good and fucked, her heart nearly giddy.

She shook her head as she brushed her teeth. She yanked on a tank and boxers from the drawer, and collapsed in bed. *Sweet exhaustion.* Three minutes later she was in dreamland.

CHASE STRETCHED GENTLY, not wanting to wake Samantha. Last night, the chatting, the dancing, and especially the sex were beyond his wildest dreams. Samantha brought out something in him he hadn't felt in a long time.

He'd slept like he'd been hibernating.

She slept so quietly.

He smiled and turned to her side of the bed.

His smile fell.

No Samantha.

He glanced toward the bathroom.

The door stood wide open.

He grabbed his shorts from the floor and slipped them on to head downstairs.

No lights on, no sounds, zero signs of Samantha.

Sonuvabitch!

The woman had snuck out in the middle of the night.

He wanted to punch something. The mail from the previous day sat in front of him on the counter. One swipe of his hand, and he sent it sailing.

Chase sucked in a deep breath through his nostrils. He'd never been a one-night-stand kind of guy. He was always the man to offer breakfast the next morning, escort the lady home. Never just a one-and-done.

He felt so used. Which didn't match anything he'd assumed about Samantha.

Patience. He just needed to exercise some patience. After all, weren't the toughest nuts to crack the tastiest? Chase never expected life to be easy. Nothing ever was. At least, nothing worth having.

But from the memory of her body beneath his, how responsive, how wild and free she made him feel, maybe his analogy was wrong. Samantha wasn't a tough nut.

She was a Calypso, strong minded, nearly untamable, and impossible to resist.

SAM JERKED AWAKE when something shoved against her shoulder.

Or someone.

"What are you doing here?"

Jordan's silhouette darkened the otherwise blinding sunlight coming in from the window.

"What time is it?" she asked.

"Ten. I let you sleep. I thought you would've spent the night with Chase." Her tone was soft, but concerned.

Sam growled and yanked a pillow over her head, to drown out the world.

"Did things not go well?"

Things went exceptionally well. "Why are you so nosy?"

"Why are you so cagey? You panicked again, didn't you?"

Yes. But at least it was after *the best sex of my life. Progress.*

The silence dragged on between them.

Jordan's heavy sigh nearly made the mattress sink. "He really likes you, woman. I thought you really liked him."

"I do. But this is vacation." She yanked the pillow off her head. "No attachments, right? Morning-after coffee and breakfast just felt too . . . awkward."

"You are many things, Samantha Callahan. But a coward isn't one of them. How was it? Tell me surfer-boy is as good in bed as he is on the waves."

The memory of last night flooded her mind. Pushing her against the door, unfurling her hair, his mouth on her body, multiple shattering orgasms . . . heat flooded her face. "Better."

Jordan chuckled, and then ripped the covers down. "Then . . . what are you waiting for?"

Sam frowned. "What?"

"Get your ass back over there, with an apology, and blow him away. Figuratively, speaking. Literally . . . well, I'm sure he won't mind if that's your gift. I'd suggest breakfast."

She smirked. "But what about you two? What do we have planned?"

"Don't worry about what we're doing. You've found your stress relief."

"This is a *girl's* week. What does that say, abandoning my two best friends for more vacation sex?"

Jordan grinned. "About damn time."

A QUICK TEN mile run didn't ease Chase's frustration. He'd never been ditched like that before, even though he could understand some of Samantha's insecurities. But it had been hours since she left, and he knew the ladies next door were awake by now. Through the kitchen window on his return home, he'd clearly seen Sam wiping down the counters.

Be patient. She needs time.

But his patience was wearing thin. And he was known for his truckloads of patience.

"Seriously, who does that?" He scraped his fingers along his scalp in the shower, even the six-foot swells in the ocean not alluring enough to expel his anxiety.

As he dressed, his doorbell chimed. He exhaled. *Samantha.*

He threw on a clean shirt, and quick dash of cologne. She was finally ready to face him after running out, and he was going to make her work for it.

When he threw open the door, a delivery guy stood on his porch.

"Delivery for Mr. Bradshaw?"

Chase's heart sank.

Until the man held up a long tube.

Then his spirits rose a bit. "Finally." He signed for the package, and read the label. From the architect designing the ASD living center. *His* center.

He opened the container, and unrolled the plans over his kitchen peninsula. Braden, his architect, included a handwritten note.

Here are the changes you wanted. I'll meet you at the site at 3pm.

Chase knew Braden would go over the schematics more in depth when they met, but he couldn't help himself from digging into them now. Unfortunately, he knew just enough to be dangerous.

The first page detailed the front elevation—the facade, windows, roofline. The second page showed side and back views. Next he turned to a birdseye view of the interior—classrooms, bathroom, halls, closets, electrical and HVAC. He wasn't sure if the lobby was spacious enough, but maybe that's something he should discuss with Braden.

A knock on his back door stole his attention.

Samantha.

He glanced at his watch, two-twenty. He opened the door and stepped back to let her in.

"Hi."

"Hi."

She glanced down before making eye contact. Her hair was pulled back again, but more loose, relaxed. Her oversized sunglasses perched on her head, keeping back stray strands. The black spaghetti-strap top hugged her curves tastefully, revealing her smooth shoulders. Dark shorts gave her an almost clandestine aura. Still adorable.

He hoped she wasn't there to tell him to take a hike.

He stood a good six-feet from her, giving her time to gather her thoughts.

"I wanted to come by, and . . . apologize."

Okay, that's a start. "For what, exactly?" He started crossing his arms, but stopped. He had to stay open. *Appear open.*

She smoothed her lips together. "For leaving in the middle of the night."

"I see. Did you not enjoy last night?"

Her eyes widened. "No! That's not it at all," she pleaded. "I had an amazing time, at the party, and . . . especially alone with you," she finished softly.

He took a step closer. "Then why didn't you stay?"

She shrugged her shoulder, looking so very un-Sam-like. And yet, he suspected, feeling very Samantha. Possibly in unchartered territory.

He closed the gap between them, and took her hands in his. "Samantha, I'm guessing what we're sharing during this brief time together is new to you."

She nodded. "I'm not that kind of girl, Chase. One night stands aren't my thing."

Hallelujah. "Mine either. Please know this, I like you. I like spending time with you. *A lot.* I won't push you more than you're comfortable with," *much,* "but when I woke to an empty bed, I thought I'd done something wrong."

She sighed. "You didn't."

"I don't want to make you run off again. But, for the remaining few days you're here, will you stay with me? Sleep in my bed, and we'll just enjoy each other?" He lifted her chin with a finger.

Her chest rose subtly, and her irises lit up. But she didn't say anything.

He leaned forward to place a gentle kiss on her lips,

slowly, giving her time to object. When she leaned in to meet him, he held her lips against his for a few seconds longer, relishing her taste. "Let me hold you, and make you feel good."

Fuck! If he had time, he'd start now and show her exactly what he was talking about. The way her eyes looked at him, practically begging him, he had to put on the brakes. More time for that later.

He kissed her again and smiled. "Come 'ere. I want to show you something."

Chapter
THIRTEEN

SHE CROSSED HER arms over her stomach. *Did I just agree to stay with him the rest of my vacation?*

Her subconscious jumped for joy. *Yes, you did.*

She forced her inner playboy bunny to calm down. Chase knew she was only here for a few more days at most. So, there really was no risk for him. Reading anything more into his request was pointless.

Chase motioned with his head toward the kitchen where large papers draped over the countertop. "I've been waiting on these forever." He grinned down at her.

She moved closer, resting a hand on her hip. From the paper's blue lines and official seals on the bottom, they were blueprints for some floor plan.

"Is this for that center you're building?"

"Mm-hm." Pride and child-like excitement radiated off him. "Three long years in the making. This is the residence wing," he pointed to a prominent outline on the plans. "Each floor will have two kitchens, and separate rooms for two full-time attendants. Educational wing is over here for trade skills, college credit courses, and general life skills. Medical facilities over here," he motioned to an area on the other side of a large garden area. "We'll have a full time doctor and nurse on staff, along with several behavioral therapists, speech and language therapists, so they can receive their treatments on campus in a safe environment. Movie theater, gym, community areas to emphasize social skills . . . "

The more he spoke, the more excited he became. Sam couldn't help but smile at his enthusiasm. She envied his passion. A passion she once had for her job. Before it became more of an effort to prove her seriousness as a woman, to a senior board of all men.

His smile widened when he finished.

"This is impressive."

"Only place like it in the whole state. A real chance."

She swung an arm around his waist. "I'm sure your sister is very proud of you."

He turned, and leaned his elbow on the counter, dripping with incalculable magnetism. His confidence was so appealing as was the slight recklessness about him.

This is why I agreed to stay with him. This natural draw and excitement . . . I actually feel alive.

He cupped her face. Then kissed her. In front of his life's work, surrounded by an air of possibilities.

She wrapped her arms around his shoulders, squeezing his tight muscles under her fingers. His minty mouthwash tasted sweet and fresh.

"Come see it with me," he said against her lips.

If he keeps kissing me like this, I'll agree to anything. "Right now? At the construction site?"

He nodded once, and gently licked the corner of her mouth. "That is, unless you have a problem with getting a little dirty."

Sam inhaled his heady cologne, and leaned into his kiss. This time, there was nothing hesitant in her grip on his shirt. "Dirty you say?"

He grinned like the devil he was, and waggled his eyebrows at her.

In front of his vision on paper, in the arms of a self-confident, sexy man, Sam wondered if she'd met her match.

Sam shaded her eyes from the sun, overlooking the impressive view of the ocean from the empty lot. The large acreage occupied the sole undeveloped coastal property in the county.

All owned by Chase.

He stood in the middle, surrounded by four men in business attire from the architecture firm.

But not her surfer-boy.

Chase wore a T-shirt and loose jeans. Casual and comfortable.

Yet he commanded all the other men's respect. From their docile body language and constant attention, they doted on him as though puppies to a master.

The longer they spoke, the less excited Chase appeared.

From his crossed arms and fading smile, he didn't like what he heard.

Eventually, he left the grouping in the middle of the parcel, and strolled over beside her, holding onto his scowl.

"You've got stellar taste, Bradshaw. This is the perfect spot to retire."

He grunted, and stared out over the water.

"Let me guess. You said jump, and instead of saying 'how high,' they said 'it'll cost extra.'"

Chase sighed. "It's not the money."

"Creative differences?"

"Permit delays."

Sam frowned. "How long?"

"Not sure. Seems as though there's some political push back."

"What's political about an ASD center?"

Something bitter crossed his face, and he took a few steps closer to the edge of the property. He kicked at a rock, sending it over the fifteen foot drop to the rocky shore below.

"Some wealthy homeowners a few miles away are pressuring city council members and the commerce board to block the permits. Concerned about their property values, with developmentally delayed *homeless* taking over the area." He nearly spit out the last sentence as if choking on phlegm.

Sam's eyes widened. "Are you shitting me?"

"It's a complete misconception. These people are not a menace. They need *help*. They are just like you and me, and everyone else sitting on their *entitled* board positions and pedestals. They deserve the same care and consideration as everyone else. All they need is a chance."

"You don't have to justify this to me. I think it's a beautiful idea. With one look at this place, I'm sure everyone else will be just as supportive."

He tilted his head. "I've spoken to the city council members so many times already. They were all on board, until these few residents started hollering."

Sam inhaled the strong breeze offshore, and let the salty air rejuvenate her mind. "I assume you've reached out to the national Autism organizations for their support and reference letters. A push for another round of those can't hurt."

Chase nodded, but the creases in his forehead didn't go away.

"Sleep on it," she suggested. "Then we can brainstorm."

"We?"

She pressed her lips together. *Maybe I overstepped.* "Only if you want to."

He removed his sunglasses, and studied her. "Samantha, I'd like that."

She felt a slight hesitation in him that made her believe he had something more he wanted to say.

"Let's go grab a bite, then I want to take you someplace."

A thrill shot through her. Standing so close, his subtle cologne in the air, there was no place she'd rather be. "Okay."

Chase held her hand as they walked from the car to the restaurant. Sam tucked her head to hide her smile. When was the last time a man had held her hand?

The restaurant was further inland, a quaint little place known for, according to Chase, their great shrimp dishes.

"You had some shrimp on the boat. You like seafood, yes?"

She smiled up at him. "Yes."

Chase ordered a bottle of some yummy Napa white, she'd never heard of the vineyard, and the shrimp sampler platter for two.

The plate had everything one could desire and more—shrimp *fra diavolo*, garlic and butter shrimp, chile shrimp, and a battered shrimp that made Sam moan when it hit her mouth.

Chase chuckled. "Good?"

"Divine," she strung out the word. "Simply divine. This was a great idea."

"Thanks. This is just our first stop."

She tilted her head. He had something up his sleeve. And she was game for whatever he wanted.

"This center of yours . . ." She leaned into the table, swirling the almost empty wine glass in her hand. "What made you decide to do it?"

He gave her a confused look. "I told you, my sister."

"Of course. But there are more than just a few ways to help those in need. Why this project?"

He sighed. "You're wondering why I don't subdivide and sell off a prime piece of real estate on the coast, instead of creating a not-for-profit charity." The hint of defensiveness in his voice matched his slightly narrowed gaze.

She blinked. "No. Why? Did someone ridicule you for that?"

The corner of his mouth lifted in a sardonic smile. "Only every single colleague I have, including my lawyer."

"Well, they're wrong. So, kudos to you for doing it despite." She downed the rest of her wine.

He chuckled, and picked up the bottle, offering to pour more into her glass.

Sam nodded, and he filled it halfway.

"The place is a beautiful vision. It came from somewhere," she prodded softly.

He cupped his glass, holding it between his long fingers, staring at the legs dripping against the sides. Several seconds passed before he finally answered. "A promise to my mother."

"This was her dream?"

"She made me promise to take care of Reese. Which, of course, I would. I have. But Mom asked me for one more thing." The grief in his voice came through clearly. He cleared his throat, and took another sip of wine. "People talked about donating to cancer research in her name, but she was adamant. She looked straight at me from that hospital bed, and said if I had the means, I was to devote them to helping those like Reese. We'd seen so many ASD kids throughout my sister's treatment who were forced to quit because they didn't have the finances, and insurance wouldn't cover it for one bullshit reason or another. Killed my mom every time."

Sam's throat went dry as sympathy weighed down her heart.

"When she passed," he continued, "we instructed everyone who insisted on donating to give to a special needs foundation. Then, we waited years for the right piece of property to go on sale. And used the funds to buy the land and start drawing up the plans. Pulled in a lot of donations and used a large chunk of my own retirement to get it off the ground."

"And here you are."

He shrugged a shoulder. "Took me long enough."

She reached across the table and slipped her fingers in his hand as she remembered a phrase from Jordan. "Those who move mountains begin with a single stone."

His pensive stare reached straight through her body and into her heart. A slow smile spread across his face, making her stomach flutter. "Confucius. Or is that a proverb?"

"I heard it from Jordan, who probably got it from an Internet meme."

He laughed. "Well, whoever said it, I like it. Along the lines of it doesn't matter how long you take, as long as you don't stop."

She grinned. *Very true.* That thought seemed to have defined her life.

"You ready for the next adventure?" he asked.

"Bring it on."

After dinner, Chase drove back toward Santa Cruz, passed the University and through downtown to Santa Cruz Beach Boardwalk.

Sam laughed. "Oh my gosh. I've heard about this."

Chase parked in the closest spot he could find. "Yup, the iconic amusement park on the beach. Let's go."

They opted not to go on any rides, which made Sam only too happy since she overindulged during dinner. Why not, she was on vacation.

"The girls would love this place."

"Bring them here tomorrow," he suggested. "The weekends get pretty packed, but it's still worth it."

CHASE SLIPPED HIS hand through hers as they walked the boardwalk. It was a gorgeous night, the high heat from the day dissipated.

"What was your job before?" she asked. She was

compelled to know more. Sam couldn't explain it, especially since she was leaving in three days. What did it matter? Who knew? Maybe they could be friends on social media, or he could come to San Fran and visit her. Santa Cruz was only an hour away.

"You mean before becoming a surfer-boy?"

She chuckled. "Yes."

"Well, you know I was in commercial real estate development. I pitched corporate retail investments in larger developments, like resorts, corporate headquarters, even a casino once, all over the world."

Her eyebrows rose. *The confidence he must have.*

"I was at the height of my career, when my boss needed me to pitch the biggest deal in our company's history." He shook his head. "I made the choice, closed the deal, but missed my sister's high school graduation. After that, my boss offered me whatever job I wanted. I chose retirement."

"Whoa. I had no idea. Now you're setting up a living community for people with ASD?"

"That's about it."

She nodded. "Impressive, Bradshaw."

He grinned.

"You traded in silk suits and ties for swim trunks and a philanthropy hat?"

"You thought I was an unemployed bum?" He chuckled.

"No." *Yes,* she hid her embarrassment. "Before the

yacht party, I thought you were a bartender."

This time, he outright laughed. "Living on the beach in Santa Cruz?"

She shrugged. "With some wicked surfing skills, and a killer smile." She tightened her hold on his arm.

The sun dipped below the horizon, leaving the sky a watercolor of pinks and blues, fading into purples and indigos. They aimlessly followed the boardwalk.

"See that lighthouse there?" He pointed to a tall, white tower in the distance. "Can you walk a mile in those shoes?"

"You bet I can. These wedges were made for walking."

She was thoroughly intrigued by this town. Jordan had done a great job of setting up the whole vacation. Of course, having Chase as her personal tour guide helped tremendously. Sam could definitely see returning some day.

As they moved closer to the lighthouse, the crowds thinned. She almost felt like she and Chase meandered around on their own private island, with the moon shining above just for them.

They made the long walk out to the lighthouse, intimidating and charming at the same time. The light at the top was already lit with three windows as a guide up the spiral staircase.

"Be careful," Chase tightened his grip on her hand.

Large, jagged rocks surrounded the paved pier. A sharp and dangerous climb, but she couldn't resist the challenge.

On a whim, she walked to the gray door and turned the

handle. It opened.

"Shit," she hissed out, and quickly shut it.

"Did that door just open?" Chase reached her in another six steps.

He turned the knob, and his eyes widened. He grinned with the mischief of a toddler. He pushed the door open, and called out if anyone was there. When no one responded, he yanked her in after.

"Oh, no. We can't be in here." Her voice bounced around the cavernous space.

With the exception of the light above and moonlight filtering in through the windows, shadows danced around the dark room.

"C'mon," he called to her as he headed for the spiral stairs.

"Oh, crap." *He's really going up there?* "Wait up."

They climbed the staircase, winding their way to the top.

"Watch the light," Chase cautioned when they reached the top.

The circular platform oversaw a sea of blackness that was the water. To the left, colorful lights from the rides on the boardwalk sparkled. The people looked like miniature, moving figurines, their laughter distant echoes on the sea breeze.

The moon appeared closer from up here, big and bright with thin wisps of clouds sketching their way across the sky.

The bright light from the spinning lens lit up her back, warming her skin instantly. Her shadow filled the beam across the water.

She held her breath. People would notice figures traipsing around the top of the lighthouse. "Chase, we should go down."

"One thing first," he replied softly. He pulled her in, and wrapped his arms around her lower back. His face nearly glowed in the light, bringing out the green and grays in his normally blue irises. He tilted his head, and pressed a gentle kiss to her lips. Skimming with his tongue, just a sweet taste. "I've always wanted to do that from up here."

She caught her breath, and licked her lips. "Was it worth it?"

He smiled. "Hell, yes."

Chase took her hand, and proceeded down the stairs. "So, this is the week for new things?" he called from her back.

When the blowjob in the car flashed in her mind, she blushed. "Yes, indeed."

Quite a few firsts.

"I have an idea of another first."

She reached the bottom, an open area with a black and white tiled floor and an office set up at the far end. She spun around to face him. "What's that?"

He approached her, his devilishly handsome face mere inches from hers. "Have you ever made love in a lighthouse?"

Chapter FOURTEEN

SAMANTHA'S STUNNED FACE when he dropped his little bomb about making love in the lighthouse was priceless. She looked positively adorable when she heard something unexpected. Which was quickly becoming one of his favorite things to do. Surprise her.

He strode a few feet to the door and locked it.

"Oh, no, Chase." She shook her head.

He returned, placing his hands on her hips and butterfly kisses on her neck. "No? Well, I think we should change that."

"That's not exactly what I meant." She tilted her head and leveled him a look.

He stepped close and reached behind to gently pull her ponytail loose. "No one will know. Even if someone might hear or get a glimpse through that window, wouldn't it be thrilling?" He placed small kisses against her tender cheeks as he let his fingers tangle in her long hair.

After a beat, a small smile graced her mouth. "I *am* on vacation."

Slowly her body melted into his, her arms closing in around his neck, giving in to the freedom and excitement of being alone in a new place.

He relished this side of Samantha. She was the type of woman who, when she made up her mind, was all in. His challenge was to convince her she should be *all in* with him.

His kisses trailed down to her shoulder, pushing against the spaghetti straps of her top.

Her breathing came stronger. She lowered his hands to his waist, letting him pull down both sides of her top to her waist.

Her breasts instantly spilled out, bared naked to him.

Fuck! "No bra, Samantha?"

"It has . . . um, one built in."

He closed his hands around her gorgeous globes and sucked a hard nub into his mouth.

She arched her back, begging for more.

He obliged as he worked on loosening her shorts.

Her hands drifted under his shirt, caressing his abs and exploring his torso.

Lower. His dick hungered for her touch.

As if hearing his thoughts, she unfastened his shorts.

He yanked a condom from his back pocket.

Over his boxer briefs, she cupped him, stroking him to new heights of hardness.

Had he ever wanted a woman as much as her?

A groan escaped his mouth just before he captured

hers. Their tongues danced, and lust coursed through his veins. He stepped out of his shorts, and backed her up against the desk. Then he pushed all the fabric off her hips.

She yelped.

He froze and looked to her face. "What?"

"This metal desk is freezing," she said with a grin.

"Soon, you won't even notice." He lowered before her and held onto her shorts. "Lift."

She took her feet out, and stood with her legs apart.

His hands grazed over her thighs, the smell of her arousal calling to him. He slid a lone finger through her slit, and her eyes fluttered. She was so wet, he'd bet he could make her come twice.

He kissed her low-belly and moved to his destination. Her folds separated when he licked up her center.

She moaned and leaned back, her hands gripping the opposite side of the desk.

He lapped more, slowly adding more pressure to her engorged clit. With two fingers, he pushed inside her, stroking her front wall.

"Oh, God, Chase."

Her voice was like music to his ears. She moaned and swayed, pushing against him, as her muscles gripped his fingers.

"Ah. Ah."

Chase glanced up fast enough to see her beautiful face as her orgasm rocked through her. He ripped open the condom pouch. He had to get inside her before his dick exploded.

Resting on the desk, Samantha stretched out her arms, beckoning him closer.

He stepped between her thighs, and she hooked her feet over his backside.

Poised at her entrance, he eased into her warmth. *Christ!*

"Samantha," he whispered against her lips, "you are beautiful when you come. I could do that over and over, for eternity." He dove completely into her as he captured her moans with his kiss.

His arms wrapped around her, pulling her flush, kissing her deeply. She was perfect for him. They were perfect together.

He slid his hand between them, and circled her eager clit.

She panted. "God, Chase. Don't stop."

He desperately needed to come, but he had to wait for her. To show her how good they were together.

"Lean back on your elbows, baby."

She did, allowing him better access with his fingers.

Bending forward, he captured one deliciously hard nipple in his mouth. Her breasts jostled as they moved, but he only sucked harder.

"Unh." She started her slow climb to ecstasy.

He claimed the other nipple, not relenting.

Samantha's heels dug into his thighs. "Chase, ah." She moaned as her head fell back, and she worked her body against his. In their very short time together, he'd never seen her so uninhibited. She took his breath away.

She screamed at the height of her orgasm.

As his balls drew up, Chase went off like a rocket, gushing everything he had inside of her.

He braced himself with one hand on the desk, and another wrapped around his girl—both of them gasping to regain breath.

"That was amazing," her voice barely a whisper.

"Yes, it was."

He didn't want to alarm her, but with her scream, they best get the hell out fast in case someone heard and came to check it out.

He pecked her lips one last time, then retrieved her shorts and handed them over. He balled up the condom in tissues from the desk, keeping a watchful eye on the window. He righted his clothes, and glanced her way.

She smiled, her face a soft rosy glow. "Maybe we should get out of here before we're discovered."

He winked and took her hand. Slowly opening the door, he peered out to check if anyone was nearby. He exhaled. Nobody that he noticed.

Samantha followed him out, and he tugged the door closed behind them.

They grinned at each other and walked back to the

boardwalk. He scattered kisses across her knuckles, and held hands the whole way.

Samantha stopped short as she gasped.

"What is it?" His eyebrows pulled together.

"I left my ponytail holder back in the lighthouse."

He stared at her, imagining the look on the guard's face when he'd walk in in the morning, wondering how it got there.

That put a smile on his face.

Samantha's expression softened, and she bit her lip trying to hold back a smile.

He wouldn't hold back anymore, and chuckled. "I do love the sex hair on you."

They both laughed, but kept walking toward his car. He couldn't wait to take her back to his place and hold her all night.

Chapter FIFTEEN

SAM OPENED THE back sliding door to their rental house, feeling beyond spent and her body fully relaxed. Her hair fell into a crazy mess and her clothes damp from a full day, and she couldn't care less.

A quick glance around proved her roomies weren't yet awake.

Time for a shower.

She blasted the water on high and stripped out of her clothes. A tinge of pain shot in her nether parts and she knew the reason—Chase.

She smiled as her body soaked under the spray.

The man was simply a sex fiend. He'd taken her back to his place, and as agreed she'd spent the night. What she hadn't counted on was his gentle coaxing and caressing, making her nearly pant with need at one in the morning. Her body still tingled with his warmth as he consumed her. *And oh, those magical fingers.*

She soaped her skin, truly appreciating the view as Chase saw her. She wasn't dissatisfied with her curvy body, she just hated knowing men saw her for her tits and ass, instead of the cleverness of her brain.

Chase seemed to cherish both sides of her, body and mind.

A few minutes later, fresh clothes on and her wet hair braided, she made her way to the kitchen for coffee. The second she turned the corner, the undeniable scent of bacon bombarded her senses. Her mouth instantly watered.

Jordan looked up from over the stove, and her eyes widened. "What are you doing back?"

Sam stared at her like she'd lost her mind. "A girl's gotta eat."

"The man doesn't feed you?" Liddy asked while pouring three cups of coffee.

"I wanted to eat with you guys. I've neglected you both so much. What's for breakfast?"

"Eggs, bacon, and toast."

Sam crawled on top of a breakfast barstool. "Smells yummy. If you weren't such an awesome gymnastics coach, you could restart your career as a chef."

"Should we tell her we don't have enough? Force her back over to surfer-boy's house." Liddy winked, and handed her a cup.

"You're that desperate to get rid of me? Do I smell bad? I just took a shower." She sipped.

"Now that you mention it . . . " Jordan wrinkled her nose.

"Liddy, you're closer. Smack her for me."

"We were expecting you to smell like sex."

Heat flooded her cheeks, which she tried to hide behind her mug.

Jordan smiled and pointed with her spatula. "Seriously, you're all relaxed. Your face has a good-and-fucked look to it."

"Jordan! Filter!" Her head dipped to hide her crazy smile. Every muscle ached. The good kind, with the promise of more to come. So the question remained, when to tell her friends about the agreement she'd made with Chase?

"What's the plan for today?"

Jordan plated the eggs as Liddy sat next to Sam. "We're renting jet skis."

"Sounds fun. And for later tonight?"

"Probably watching *Steel Magnolias*." Jordan settled on a barstool.

"For the millionth time," Liddy added, her eyes skyward. "But if I can get through that, then she has to sit through *Death Race*," Liddy said with a grin.

Sam chuckled and drove her fork into the eggs. "Would you be up for going to Breakwater again? Chase has to help out there tonight."

"You mean more dancing, and hot guys? Sounds like fun." Jordan shared a look with Liddy.

"What?" Sam asked. She glanced between the two.

Liddy leaned closer, like she had a secret to share. "She

thinks you and Chase are like a love story."

"No one is calling this . . . this *thing* with Chase a love story."

"*I* sure as hell am," Jordan corrected.

All heat vanished from her cheeks. *Love? I don't think so.*

"It's all over your face, Sam." Jordan set down her fork. "Honest-to-God love. Whether it's a long-term love or just for this week, who knows? But it's love."

Oh dear God. "That's not what this trip is about." Her tongue started to swell.

"But that's what it's become. And when that love comes, girl, you just have to take it and run with it. Full-steam-ahead, one-hundred percent, like you do with your job."

Her mouth turned dry, and she swallowed more coffee. Suddenly, her heart thundered like a stampede of Clydesdales.

"I know you're scared." Jordan's tone softened. "But do you want to know how I'm sure this is better than what you shared with Lance?"

"How?" she asked hesitantly.

Jordan grabbed the phone from out of the kitchen drawer and held it up. "You haven't touched this sucker for two days. You haven't even *asked* where I put it."

Sam blinked. Jordan was right. She hadn't checked to see if the client's presentation had been scheduled, or for any kind of response from her boss. Even now, as she sat here questioning this connection with Chase, she had no urge—at least not strong—to check the device that had once been another appendage.

"You've found a new passion, Sam." Jordan set down the phone. "Give yourself some time to figure that out here. Bask in it, soak your fingers in it until they prune. At least escape your old routine."

Liddy covered Sam's hand with hers. "We all know you love your job like Jordan loves gymnastics, or happy hour. But all work and no play makes Jane a robot."

"Exactly," Jordan added, with a side glare at Liddy. "Rude comments aside, you were using your career as an excuse not to let other people in. Like, an anti-Lance addiction. Chase seems to be the cure."

Sam sighed. "Ah, shit."

"What?" Liddy asked.

"I hate it when you're right." She crunched on a strip of bacon. "You'll never let me live it down now."

Jordan chuckled. "Why?"

"'Cuz Chase already asked me to stay with him the rest of the week."

Liddy started laughing, and had to set down her cup. "Are you serious?"

Sam blushed, and arranged the food on her plate.

"Well, then," Jordan winked. "You really are the queen of sales. Eat up, buttercup. I have a feeling you'll need the energy."

CHASE'S BREATH LODGED in his throat the second Samantha walked through the door at Breakwater with her friends. Her white jean skirt hugged her hips like a second skin. The pink hibiscus on her top complemented her tanned skin. Once again, her hair was pulled back away from her face. The sun added highlights to her hair that women paid big bucks to top stylists for the same effect.

Their gazes met.

She smiled.

Fuck me! Total stunner.

A cool sensation running over his fingers made him look down. He cursed under his breath. Overfilled the beer glass, again. Thankfully, David was too busy to notice.

Samantha leaned her elbows against the bar. "Hello, surfer-boy."

The way she said his nickname made him pine for later tonight. "Hello, gorgeous. What can I get you?"

"Three screaming orgasms, please," she said with a gleam in her eye.

Oh yes, Samantha's barrier was slowly coming down. "That's a promise. And what would you like to drink?"

She grinned from ear to ear. "We're gonna pace ourselves and start with three light beers."

"Comin' right up."

As he popped the caps off the longnecks, he met her vibrant stare. "You look beautiful tonight. The beach agrees with you."

"Thank you."

"I get off at eleven, but David said if he slows up, he'll let me go early. So, you coming over later?"

The smallest hint of pink tinted her cheeks. "Yes."

He set the beers on napkins and slid them her way. "Good, I can't wait." He winked and headed to a couple vying for his attention.

He glanced Samantha's way throughout the night. Sometimes catching her looking at him. The girls danced a bit, shared a plate of appetizers, and drank beer.

There was something incredibly satisfying knowing Samantha was nearby, in the same room, even if he couldn't talk to her.

The knowledge that they hadn't discussed Friday or any plans after she'd leave wasn't lost on him. Samantha had told him they had the place until Friday morning, and the keys had to be turned in by eleven. But if she wasn't expected back at work on Friday, why couldn't she stay with him? He could drive her back to San Fran Sunday afternoon.

After that, they could take turns, visiting each other on alternating weekends. At least until she was ready for the next step.

Maybe that night he could broach the subject, coax her into at least thinking about seeing each other after this week. Because he knew for sure, Samantha was exactly who he wanted to spend the rest of his life with. She might just need more time coming to that same conclusion.

Chase glanced at the door, and his jaw nearly dropped to the floor. Walking in was none other than Miles Terrence, the city councilmember leading the effort against his ASD center. *My ASD center.*

The man normally carried a pompous air about him, but tonight he was a tad less self-important and more reserved, while he led his wife into the room. The hostess escorted them to a seat in the back. Miles's silvery hair looked darker in the lighting, but he wore an honest-to-God tacky Hawaiian shirt.

Chase had researched this man thoroughly during the initial permit request to city council. He was a ruthless businessman in pharmaceuticals, but bended like a rubber dog toy when it came to his wife. Obviously, the choice in attire had to be her influence.

David whistled from across the bar. He motioned with his chin to Miles in the corner, and Chase nodded. Roxie came over with their drink orders, a strawberry margarita and whiskey and ginger ale.

David got to work on the margarita machine, and murmured under his breath, "Did you invite him?"

"Of course not."

"He wouldn't set foot in here unless there was a reason."

"Or his wife wanted it," Chase corrected.

"Do you need me to take care of them tonight?" His

friend's concerned expression didn't relieve any of Chase's anxiety.

David was one of the few friends he'd shared this turmoil with regarding the center. Mainly because he was a great sounding board with a countenance of Fort Knox. Any conversation with David stayed with him.

As if on cue, Miles's survey of the room landed on Chase. A flicker of a scowl crossed his face, until he realized Chase stared right back. He smiled politely, and even waved.

"I'm gonna take a five," Chase tossed at David. His friend nodded absently.

Might as well tackle this head on.

He strolled over with their drinks and set them on the table. "Miles, good to see you."

"I forgot you were moonlighting here," his rough voice countered his smooth words. "Jillian was craving fish and chips."

Chase smiled through the irony. Not to knock on his friend's business, but there were a dozen places around here that offered the traditional bar food. "Well, I'm glad she was, and you chose Breakwater. This first round is on me."

The thin woman's eyes widened in surprise, but Miles waved his hand. "You know I can't accept gifts from those with pending permit requests. It starts with a few drinks or dinner, and then it grows to bigger ticket items, like vacations and cars."

It was hard not to laugh in the man's face. "It's just two

drinks. I vow here and now I will never buy you dinner, let alone a car or vacation." Even harder was not to snort.

Miles's smile was almost pained. "I'd rather not."

"Very well. Your wife's drink is free. Not yours." He grinned, getting a kick out of playing with him.

Jillian burst into laughter. Several people around them stopped and stared, but she kept on laughing, until she almost cried. "Ease up, darling. It's my first drink in eighteen months." She looked at Chase. "I accept, and thank you."

"Eighteen months?" he asked. "What cruel and unusual punishment kept you from delicious margaritas for so long?"

"Chemo," she said it like a curse word. "Here's to remission." She held up her glass in a toast.

Miles's expression turned tender and heartfelt for his wife, but with an edge of discomfort.

Several bystanders lifted their glass to her, with a few 'here here's' scattered around them—including Sam, Jordan, and Liddy a few tables over.

Chase grinned.

His first instinct was to make sure the woman didn't pay for a single thing all night, as well as announce to the whole restaurant they had a bonafide survivor in their presence. But from her husband's obvious unease with the spotlight, he respected the pair enough to refrain.

"Massive congrats to you," he replied, and took their food order.

On his way back to the bar, he caught Sam's smiling

gaze and winked.

Over the next hour, several people came up to the bar asking to pay for Jillian's meal and drinks. The generosity of patron after patron warmed his heart. That's why he loved this community. Their hearts were huge when they saw the person behind the gift. When they saw what they were donating to, first hand.

Despite his wife battling her own fight with cancer, Miles had pushed back so hard on the ASD center without an ounce of compassion. A few more puzzle pieces fit together on why, but it still didn't add up. How to get the man to change his mind?

As the night's entertainment started in the corner, a popular DJ from San Jose, the pair finished their meal and stood to leave. Chase smiled and waved as they walked out. He went back to fixing drinks, before Miles called out to him from the end of the bar.

He finished pouring a beer for someone, and came over. "Everything all right?"

"I want to thank you for doting on her tonight."

"Of course. Congrats, by the way. That's not an easy fight." A lump crawled into his throat, thinking of his mother. Who'd lost her battle.

"No, it hasn't been. But I also wanted to ask you to keep this private."

He cocked his head. "How do you mean?"

Miles glanced around him, the discomfort obvious.

"Not many knew she had cancer. We didn't want to draw attention or pity. I would appreciate it if you wouldn't go around using this in your efforts with your . . . center."

A tinge of anger swirled in his gut. "What do you mean by 'using this'?"

"I know you're pushing really hard for that place, and I don't know if you're the kind of man who would try and use my wife's illness against me in swaying others to your cause."

All sympathy drained from his body. *The man actually thinks I would stoop that low.*

"I don't know what you're implying, Miles. But I wouldn't use cancer as a bargaining chip against anyone." It was nearly impossible to keep the disdain from his voice. "Have a good night."

Chapter SIXTEEN

CHASE LOOKED DOWN at Samantha as she stared at her plate of cold nachos.

David had given him the all-clear, and frankly, he couldn't wait to get his ass out of there.

"Interested in heading out?"

She smiled up at him. "Absolutely. Let me tell the girls." She slung her purse over her shoulder and walked to the dance floor.

Chase hung back. The girls chatted briefly and laughed. Then Liddy and Jordan looked his way and waved. He smiled back.

Chase opened his car door for her, and she settled into the seat. As he drove back to his place, he held her hand the whole way. Her warm, delicate hand inside his felt soothing. The simple act helped ease the tension that had gathered behind his eyes and in his shoulders.

"Who was that man and woman at the bar tonight? You looked like you knew them."

He ground his teeth. "That was a city councilman, Miles

Terrence, and his wife."

"Oh." She turned toward him. "Did you invite them? To try and plead your case?"

He shook his head. "They were just there for dinner."

"Did you know that about his wife? The remission?"

"No." His lips thinned.

"You'd think with his wife having her own personal medical battles, he'd be a little more open and willing to help with someone else's efforts on special needs."

"I get the feeling it's the exact opposite."

"How do you mean?"

More tension filled his shoulders. He flexed his fingers on the steering wheel to keep from gripping too tight. "I didn't know why he was pushing back so hard, until I met his wife tonight. I think he's angry. Seeing his wife suffer through cancer and needing help, that when our center was proposed to assist those with autism, maybe he resented it. '*Why are they getting help, when my wife suffers?*'"

"Like *Twelve Angry Men*, but instead of a man's son influencing his anger, it's a sick wife."

"Exactly." He inhaled through his nostrils. "It's very difficult to change the mind of someone with that kind of predisposition."

"Maybe not. We just need to find the right angle. The best way to jog your brain from a problem is change the scenery. So, that's what we'll do."

Samantha was sweet, but he didn't see an easy way out

of this mess.

He pulled into his driveway and glanced her way. "That's why I bought this place. I liked the scenery."

As they entered the dark house, Sam's attention was drawn to the moonlight skimming the water's surface. *So beautiful.*

"Want some ice water?" he asked.

"That'd be great. I'm going out to the deck."

"My place is yours," he replied.

He filled two glasses with water as Samantha went out back, and inhaled deeply. The salty air mixed with a hint of earthy incense from a few houses over. This view would never get old.

He stood beside her, handing her a glass.

She sighed. "I can see why you chose to retire early and live here."

His gaze glued to the waves beyond. "It's a little slice of paradise." Glancing her way, he said, "You could retire, too, you know."

She scoffed. "I don't think so, surfer-boy. Not yet, at least."

"Why not? You've worked hard for years. I'm sure you've got a nest egg stashed somewhere." He phrased it like a question, but someone like Samantha likely had her entire future mapped out, including retirement.

She glanced away a brief second, perhaps debating whether this was a topic she even wanted to discuss. "I'm not where I want to be in my career yet. I want a director-level position. There's this promotion opportunity just a few weeks away. I've worked my ass off toward it for years."

"What for? More money?" He persisted, gently, but he couldn't let up yet.

"Sure, the money is nice, but I want to make it, Chase. Shatter that glass ceiling. I want to show the world I can succeed. So when I walk in a room, I command respect because I've *earned* it."

"Why? Why is showing the world so important? I'm not trying to badger you, Samantha." He laid his hand over hers on the railing. "I'm merely asking because I've been there. I thought 'making it' would make me happy. Do you even like your job?"

She blinked. "I don't know. I like when the client is pleased."

Her tone of voice didn't match her words. She was reaching. "I could see the moment I laid eyes on you that you're a driven, determined woman. So much so, you went so far as to change your appearance to suit the role. You believe that to succeed in a traditionally male role, you needed to hide all that made you a woman."

She shrugged her shoulder. "You might feel the same way if you were repeatedly critiqued on what you *wore* or your makeup, but given no real accolades on your presentation. I can't tell you how many times I've been seen first as a sexual object. Femininity is a weakness in my world."

"There's a difference between being feminine and being a sexual object. You gave up the things that made you feminine for fear of being treated like a sex object or not being taken seriously."

Her eyes glinted that he may have finally given her some kernel of truth to ruminate on. "That's easy for you to say. You made it in a 'man's world.'"

"Sure, with hard work and determination. Like you. And I sacrificed to get there." He exhaled. "I agree, being judged for your clothing and makeup in a business setting is wrong. Inappropriate, and had I been in that conference room then, I would've shut down those pricks for that kind of mentality. But sacrificing who you are as a person for the standards of others . . . " He shook his head.

"Welcome to my world."

He caressed her wrist, sliding up her arm to the crook of her elbow. "You've had a lot of fun on this vacation, right?" he said with a smile.

She grinned. "Yes."

"You don't have enough fun in your life, do you?" He moved behind her, his arms bracketing her against the railing. "Because your long hours of working so hard have turned into long weeks, months, and years," he whispered in her ear as he laid a kiss just below it.

"I don't know."

Another kiss, and he reached to pull out the pins in her

hair and massage her scalp. He loved the connection, playing with her hair.

"If you don't stop to enjoy the view, you'll wake up with your life behind you, wondering where it went." He fluttered kisses along her neck, still rubbing her scalp in soft circles.

Her breath changed. Goosebumps rose on her arms.

"Behind you, right now, is a man who cherishes every single feminine thing about you."

HIS MASSAGING CONTINUED, and he pushed her hair to the side to kiss her neck again. His kisses warmed her skin, and sent tingles throughout her body. He wrapped an arm across her waist and pulled her closer. The heat from his body penetrated hers. His growing erection nestled against her ass.

Her heart hiccuped. "Chase, I don't think we should do this here."

"We definitely should. We're in complete darkness. Far enough away from the beach, if someone walks by they won't even know we're here . . . unless you make noise." The amusement in his voice sent her heart racing.

His hands slid under her top and over her abdomen. He palmed her breasts and toyed with the already-peaked nipples.

Oh damn! She dropped her head back against his shoulder and gave in to the delicious shivers jolting through her body.

Under her top, he unclasped her bra and returned his hands to her front.

"You feel so good, Samantha."

She let out a low moan, and reached her hands behind them to grab his ass.

Butterfly kisses landed on her cheeks. Then his lips whispered over her ear. "I need your help, baby. I don't want to take my hands off you. Reach into my back pocket for a condom. Hold it in your mouth and undo my pants. Can you do that?"

She would do anything he asked right then. She felt her way through her tasks.

Chase continued fondling her breasts and toying with her nipples. He tugged and twisted, and the erotic sensation shot straight to her clit.

She moaned through her gritted teeth, focusing on holding the sheath.

"Ssh," he breathed in her ear. "I think I hear voices."

She inhaled sharply, and held her breath. She didn't hear a thing, just the waves gently washing ashore.

Chase continued his merciless attention on her mounds, despite the threat of approaching intruders. But if he could stay quiet, so could she.

Reaching behind, she pushed his shorts to the ground and cupped her hand over his cock.

He growled in her ear, and his hands traveled south to her denim skirt, inching it up her hips, exposing her panties.

His fingertips played over her sex, caressed her hips, and squeezed her ass.

A shadow moved in the distance, along the shoreline. A couple arm-in-arm walked through the sand, letting the water lap at their feet. The night was too dark to see their faces, but they walked toward Chase's property.

He pinched her nipple, and she clamped her lips closed to keep from moaning.

"You make me do crazy things, Samantha. I love it," he breathed into her hair.

Oh, his words. She would miss hearing those sensual words falling from his mouth.

He skimmed his fingers over her panties, finding her little pearl.

Her body jerked and she moaned. There was no holding back that sound. But she kept her eyes on the couple, still moving up the beach. Thankfully, still unaware of their presence.

"Ssh. Do you want them to see us?" he whispered. He pulled her thong aside, and slid a finger through her wet slit.

She gasped, and widened her stance for him.

God, his touch felt so good, she wanted to moan again. She panted through her teeth, not letting the condom package drop.

He played her like a violin.

She whimpered, wanting more, needing more. A slight trickle ran down her inner thigh.

"Yes, my love?"

She couldn't respond. And he knew it. Her hands rubbed him harder, and he growled.

In a painfully slow, methodical move, he yanked her top and bra up, exposing her breasts. He cupped them, playing again with her nipples. She arched into his hands.

"My wanton baby. Do you need an orgasm?" he asked as quietly as the surf. "If my cock slid into you right now, would that help your ache?"

She whimpered, and rubbed his erection harder.

He pulled his hips back. "Oh, you bad girl. Trying to torment me. Push down my briefs."

With her stare on the oblivious pair by the water, she did as he bid and immediately grabbed his hard cock.

He took the packet from her mouth, ripped it open, and covered himself. With his hand splayed over her tummy, he inched her away from the railing a step, giving him easier access.

"Hold on."

He slammed into her before she could grab the railing tightly. Her hand flew forward and pushed her water glass off the railing, landing in the sand below with a thud.

She held her breath, letting her muscles rejoice in tightening around his length.

The couple paused just in front of his house, looking out over the water. The woman pointed to something in the distance, and kicked the seafoam.

Chase slowly moved inside her, almost as if daring the pair to turn and see them. "Fuck, Samantha, you feel incredible." His hands caressed her ass, her hips and her thighs.

She pushed back with his every stroke. "Chase." She panted. "I'm close, but I need more."

"Yes, you do." As he spoke, he took one of her hands and brought it to her pussy. With his finger over hers, he stroked up the center, dragging the wetness to her clit. "Stay here, baby, but don't come too soon."

Her heart hammered against her sternum. The brazen act of pleasing herself in front of strangers, who at any moment could turn and see her fully exposed, made her throb for even more.

His hands went back to her breasts. A moan escaped.

Pumping slowly and methodically, his fingers still pulling, twisting, and pinching. "You must be a sight, baby. Your beautiful body on display, getting pleasure in the best way possible. You don't want this to end do you?"

She bit her lip, and let her head drop forward.

"No, you don't. Neither do I." His voice was so soft, given into her ear.

The couple kept strolling down the beach, their shadows growing smaller in the dim moonlight. As her building climax grew higher every second.

"I could make love to you every day," he continued, picking up the pace. "And if you were sick, I'd nurse you back to health. I'd make you laugh, and show you the world."

What is he saying?

"We shouldn't say goodbye on Friday, should we?"

She froze.

"Don't stop, baby. Don't overthink it. I want more than a week, and I think you do, too." He moved his finger over hers again to keep her going.

She was struck by his words and didn't know what to think.

He pinched her nipple, and her clit jumped. "Think about it later, baby. Right now, you and I are going to come."

He pushed deeper inside her, and she stifled a squeal. She worked her clit harder as he increased his speed. He was close. Oh, and so was she.

As their release came like a tornado, she moaned into her shoulder, seeing stars and gasping for air. She was vaguely aware of Chase growling into her hair, whispering praises to her.

Oh, God!

The bystanders were far down the beach now, barely visible in the dark.

The thrill of that moment, on the verge of being caught, had sent her lust on overdrive. Their breathing calmed and he helped her fix her clothes, then righted his own, at least enough to collapse in a chair.

"Come here," he called to her.

She straddled his lap.

He wrapped his arms around her, and pulled her close. They dozed for a few moments before she felt him lifting her and carrying her to his bed.

He helped her out of her clothes, which didn't require much effort, and climbed in behind her.

She sighed, utterly relaxed and comfortable with Chase's body encasing hers.

His words circled in the back of her mind, but she was far too exhausted and blissfully sore to dwell on them. She'd let her rational side figure that out tomorrow. After she soaked her soul in this audaciously reckless man behind her. Who'd made her as equally reckless in less than a week.

SOMETHING WARM AND rigid slid up Sam's lower back, coaxing her awake. Dim rays of light came through the shade's edges, hidden behind thin cream curtains.

A delicious ache registered from between her legs. One she hadn't felt in ages. From days of welcome abuse and attention. From Chase.

My surfer-boy.

He wove his fingers through her silky hair, probably a mess draped across his pillow, but she didn't care. Goosebumps rose all over her body from the scalp massage. He suckled her ear lobe, his breath warm and tantalizing.

"Good morning, beautiful."

She hummed her approval. *Good morning, Adonis.*

"Sleep well?"

"And then some." She turned and slid her knee between his legs, followed by her hand reaching his hard-on. "Did this guy get any sleep last night? Or does he get overtime on the night shift?"

He chuckled. "Difficult to go to sleep when the dream

is right next to me."

Yeah, he knows how to lay it on thick.

"Are you hungry?" he asked.

"Famished."

"How about an all-I-can-eat buffet?" His smile turned devilish, and he slid down her body, never releasing his teasing eye contact until he reached her thighs.

Heat flushed her cheeks, and she couldn't help but grin. She couldn't remember the last time she'd been a feast. Thinking about it made her wet, or maybe it was just him.

His tongue tasted her slit, teasing and persistent, erasing all thoughts from her mind.

She scraped her fingers through his hair, curling her toes into the sheets.

He tucked her legs over his shoulders, and braced her ass in his hands, moving in for the long feast. His expert attention focused solely on her over-sensitive nub, sending jolts of ecstasy through her limbs.

He lapped at her like she was *crème brulee*. Hungry, and unrelenting until she screamed his name.

"Yes," he growled. Lunging for his nightstand, he pulled out another condom and slipped it on.

The orgasm's kinetic energy still pulsed through her. His ceiling fan blades blurred overhead, and multiplied as if they were spinning. Then, his face filled her vision.

She cupped his cheeks to steady herself, to get the room to stop moving.

"Keep riding that wave, Samantha." His voice was so husky. Low and feverish. His hips pushed against her thighs, and his tip found her seam. With a single thrust, he hissed out her name.

Her muscles clenched around his cock, jolting another ripple through her limbs.

"I can feel it," he said. "You're still coming."

"Yes," she moaned. She wrapped her legs around his ass, and squeezed him in. "More, don't stop."

The vibrations escalated with his pumping, constricting her lungs. Her pants became gasps. Every cell in her body nearly boiled with heat, and the tidal wave surged closer.

"That's it, sweetheart," Chase cooed. "Charge that wave until it curls and drops. Then take off."

The swell burst through her body on a wail. She curled her toes into his skin and let the rushing flow over her.

"That's it," he bellowed. "Come for me." He thrust harder, and her channel spasmed out of control.

His name came out on gasping breaths, and her face tingled. All the way down to her fingertips and toes, everything tingled.

"Do you want more?" he asked, his voice shaking.

She opened her eyes, stared into his piercing blues, now darkened to a stormy dark gray color. And nodded.

Something flashed in his gaze, and he pulled out. With a firm grip on her waist and elbow, he flipped her over, and nudged her forward on her knees.

Her breasts skimmed the sheets, her nipples hard and sensitive as they brushed against the damp fabric. Sweat glistened down her chest, and her hair felt matted against her neck.

She turned her head to look at him.

His whole body was flushed, his abs taut and glistening like hers, only incredibly defined.

Her mouth watered.

CHASE GRABBED HER hips, and pulled her ass into his frame, aligning his dick with her slick sex. Samantha was beyond wet. She was drenched . . . because of him. All for him.

He smiled at the thought. Such a gift.

As he slid inside her, he exhaled on a swear. Her body squeezed around him, holding him in this perfect, hot cocoon. He'd give everything he owned just to stay right here.

His rhythm increased slowly, with each lunge she panted out the word "yes," over and over. His body lunged faster and harder, pushing against the back of her until her knees rose up off the bed. His grip dug into her hips, desperate to remain in control.

Watching her ride those waves of an orgasm had been the hottest thing he'd ever seen. Now, he was addicted to getting her off. He craved the sound of her scream at the peak of her climax.

His thrusts grew jerky, and his sac tightened up into his body. Stars burst behind his eyelids, and he finally imploded on another growl. Moaning out her name.

He moved his hands to her breasts, holding her there as his body pitched through spilling his seed, in the greatest climax of his life.

Samantha collapsed beneath him, catching her breath.

He rolled off, careful not to crush her with his weight. His quads trembled from the exertion.

Surfing has nothing on Samantha.

"I can't feel my face," she panted.

He chuckled, and nipped at her shoulder, followed by several kisses along her creamy skin. "Nor can I feel my legs."

"Don't we make a strange pair."

God, I hope so.

"Time for a drink."

"Water, first," she pleaded. "For the love of God, water."

He laughed, stretching out the spasms in his legs. "Whatever you like."

After escaping to the bathroom to clean up and dispose of the condom, he slipped on his boxers and retreated downstairs to the kitchen.

Streaks of daffodil yellow painted the sky over the horizon outside the panoramic windows. The sea was a blanket of slate blue, the crests catching the rays of sunrise, and fading into a pearly white leading into the breaker waves that hugged the shoreline. Several miles beyond floated tiny yellow dots, sidelights from passing yachts, tankers, and cruise ships.

His favorite view on the planet.

Until Samantha tiptoed down the steps wearing his black T-shirt.

His tongue swelled, and he had to roll it back into his mouth.

Mussed hair, pink cheeks, and delectable bare legs . . .

That's my new favorite view.

"What's your beverage of choice?" she asked.

"You."

She grinned. "Good answer. But really, you know my weakness is rum punch. What's yours?"

"I thought yours was a screaming orgasm?"

She sidled up to him, and wrapped her arms around his waist. "Besides that one. If I had to guess, I'd peg you as either a whiskey man, or imported beer."

"Lucky guess. IPA." He turned and handed her a tumbler of ice water.

She thanked him and downed half the glass.

"After your plans with the girls, I'd like to take you somewhere tonight."

"Where's that?"

"It's a surprise."

"Is it another center you're building, like a homeless shelter or haven for lost puppies?"

His heart warmed. "No, I'm selfish. All my altruism

goes to just the one place."

She kissed his cheek and retreated to the table, which boasted the glamorous view of the ocean at sunrise.

They sat side by side, watching the waves roll in from the glittering water beyond. Tomorrow was her last day here. Unless he could convince her otherwise. Because now there was no doubt in his mind he wanted her to stay. Stay for good.

But after barely a week here, she would surely push back. How could he convince her that *he* was worth it?

"Not too bad, Bradshaw." She gestured to the beach view.

"The best decision I ever made," Chase sighed. "Reminds me of what's really important to me. Reese forgave me for missing her graduation, and eventually I forgave myself. I swore to never put work over my family again. I had missed out on too much of my own life. Which is probably another reason I was so drawn to you, when I first saw you."

Her head shot up.

"I recognized the corporate America mentality on you."

"You say that like it's a disease."

He turned his head to face her. "You are clearly so driven—determined—to have the world take you seriously. As if it's the only way your life can have meaning. Reminded me so much of myself."

"That's the answer," she finally announced.

"Answer to what?"

"The city council."

"I don't follow."

"Your sister. The answer to your issues with the city council is your sister." Samantha sat forward in her chair. "Have her speak to them."

He leaned closer, elbows resting on his knees. "I'm listening."

"Chase, you're one charming man," she said with a smile, "and I'm sure you've done all your homework and know all the statistics. But Miles needs a different perspective. Someone who *has* ASD, and could've benefited from a place like this. Make it personal. He saw his wife suffering first hand, and that obviously makes him sympathetic. So, let him see the *people* who need this center. The best thing about this is it's not an angle. It's real life. *That's* what he responds to."

"A testimonial." He looked out over the sea, and pursed his lips.

"You don't think Reese would be willing to do it?" she asked.

After a rough sigh, he looked at her again. "Reese can't stand public speaking, it's very nerve-racking for her. But for this . . . something to help the growing ASD population, she just might."

She smiled, and finished the rest of her water.

"You found the answer."

Sam shrugged shyly.

"I thought *I* was good at reading people. How do you do it? Are you secretly Wonder Woman?"

She winked. "Don't tell anyone."

He glided his hand to her bare thigh. "I intend to tell the world."

Chapter EIGHTEEN

SAM BREATHED IN the fresh coffee, savoring the scent before taking her first sip. Warmth smoothed her throat as Jordan came down the stairs.

The smile on her friend's face matched the joy in Sam's heart.

"Mornin', sex fiend."

Sam laughed. Then poured a second cup for her friend.

Jordan stirred in some sugar, and climbed atop the barstool next to Sam. "How was the pleasure palace?"

"Top notch." She didn't bother hiding her blush this time. "How was last night?"

"Top notch," Jordan parroted. "Danced until last call."

They tapped their mugs, and took another sip each.

After a sigh, Jordan inclined her head. "You look as happy as you did in college."

Smiling came so easy. "I am happy. This vacation has been . . . " Words failed her. *Refreshing* wasn't nearly descriptive enough, or encapsulating of how alive she felt.

"I know," Jordan replied with a grin. "Exactly what you

needed."

"I'd like to show you both the Boardwalk today."

"The amusement park? That's what you pointed out yesterday while jet skiing? Looks like fun. But, you don't have more plans with Chase?"

"Sure I do, later tonight. But I want to spend most of our last day with you two."

Jordan's smile slipped. "Have you and Chase talked about what happens tomorrow?"

Liddy clomped down the hallway, rubbing the sleep from her eyes and her hair bundled atop her head. "Coffee, please."

"Another hangover?" Sam asked.

"Oh, yes. She obliterated a bottle of Moscato all on her own."

"Well, let's make up a little hair-of-the-dog for you, because we have a fun-filled morning planned."

Liddy folded herself over a chair. "She's so exhausting when she's had sex," she grumbled.

Thirty minutes later, Liddy climbed into the car as Sam grabbed her phone from the counter. A flashing light showed several missed calls and new voicemails.

She listened to the first one. The computer repair guy, saying her laptop was fixed and running perfectly. Ready for pickup.

Great news. But nothing she was ready to rush home for. There was still a full day of vacation left.

"Sam, put down that phone, and hurry up!" Jordan called from the front door.

Finally, the towering Ferris wheel stood in front of them, with the sounds of rollercoasters and arcade games chiming in the background. The place wasn't as packed first thing in the morning, which Sam had counted on.

Somewhere after their third ride on Shockwave, they settled in for a garden burger and fried artichoke hearts at a patio restaurant inside the Boardwalk. Sam redid her ponytail, to keep her hair off her neck.

"Is that the lighthouse Chase took you to?" Liddy asked, pointing over the Ferris wheel.

"Yep." Sam's cheeks heated, remembering the incredible orgasm he'd given her on the desk. Her hair band might still be sitting there.

"You didn't answer me this morning," Jordan started, after a bite into her burger.

"What question?"

"Have you two talked about what's going to happen tomorrow? Will you see more of each other?"

Sam sighed. "Not exactly." She sipped on her fresh lemonade. "He says he wants to see me again."

"Really?" Liddy grinned. "What did you say?"

"I . . . um . . . " She hadn't had the chance to respond. He'd made her climax so hard right as he'd asked for more. "Have to think about it."

"What's to think about?" Jordan leaned back in her

seat, letting the sea breeze brush against her face. "You obviously love him."

Liddy bent forward to keep her words from anyone that might hear. "And surfer-boy is clearly good in the sack." She chuckled. "No one said you had to have a double-digit IQ to get you off."

"Actually, he's a hell of a lot more than just a surfer-boy slash bartender." Sam licked her lips.

"I figured as much," Jordan replied. "House like that on the beach, he's got a stash somewhere. Good for him. Let me guess, trust fund baby?"

Sam shook her head. "Retired real estate developer, and now working part-time as a bartender while he uses his investments to build a living community for special needs children and adults with autism."

Liddy's eyes widened, and Jordan's jaw dropped.

"Yeah, I know. Intimidating."

"You mean, just donating the money or land for it?" Jordan asked.

"No, actually overseeing the design, hiring all the staff, and fighting city hall for it. Putting his own skin in the game, because his sister has ASD."

"Jordan's right," Liddy announced.

Sam stared at her.

"What the hell is there to think about?" Liddy repeated.

Sam pressed her lips together.

"This guy makes Lance look like a deadbeat. Why are

you balking?"

"Because this isn't real life." She gestured to the Boardwalk, meaning the whole vacation. "My life is in San Francisco. There's no way this can work beyond tomorrow."

"Why not?" Jordan asked.

"He's over an hour away."

"Oh, dear Lord. How in the world do people make relationships work over such long distances?" Liddy mocked. "A whole hour? You sit in traffic longer than that."

Sam scowled at her. "I work all the time. When will I ever get to see him? Let alone give us any real chance to make it work?"

"You *make* the time," Jordan replied, as if the answer were like reading a lesson out of a children's book. "You work less, to live more."

Sam took another sip of her lemonade. The concept of working less, as enticing and awesome as it sounded, was impossible. Not if she wanted to make that next level. The level she was promised.

Because moving here was out of the question. The commute alone would disadvantage her to her peers. Getting up even earlier than she already did, and getting home later. The number of times she'd have to call and apologize for missing dinner or delaying quality time with him . . .

"Did you enjoy this week?"

"Yes, of course."

"Did you love everything about your time with him?"

"Every minute. But be realistic. It's just not feasible. The major inconvenience of that lifestyle . . . it's not fair to him. I barely see you guys as it is, and you *live* in San Fran."

Jordan shook her head. "You're making up excuses. If you really want this life with him, you'd make it work, no matter the barriers. And news flash . . . these aren't barriers. These are molehills, not mountains."

A family walked by. The two children clinging to their parents' hands carried massive smiles and tiny foam surfboard souvenirs.

"You see him again tonight?" Jordan asked.

She nodded, an ache gripping her heart all the sudden.

"Talk to him," she urged. "Don't be so quick to shut him out. He seems like a rare catch, and you should give him a chance. Since when have you ever let something as trivial as mere mileage stop you from getting what you want?"

Sam tightened her jaw.

"Besides, I've always wanted a friend who owned a beach house I could crash at every other weekend." Jordan winked.

CHASE HELD SAM'S hand as he stepped over the rough rocks leading down to Panther Beach. Each step was careful and slow, because slipping here would mean nasty scrapes.

"This place is gorgeous," Sam marveled. The sun sat

just above the horizon, casting long strokes of amber, fuchsia, and violet across the sky, hiding behind puffy white clouds.

"*You're* gorgeous." He helped her off the last rock, and pulled her against his body.

She grinned, and melded her mouth to his. The breeze blew up the skirt of her black halter dress, revealing creamy bare thighs.

He trailed his fingers down her hips to her skin.

She hummed into his mouth, and nipped his tongue. "Let's go find a cozy spot."

She kicked off her sandals, scooped them up and pulled him along the beach. The rock formations formed a wide opening to the beach, but closed off to the shoreline, giving an illusion of privacy in a rocky paradise. A small archway in the rocks led to another private sandy area, more secluded.

She led him right to it.

"I'm so glad you picked this spot," he said.

"Why's that?" She pulled the blanket from the bag he carried around his shoulder.

"This part is only revealed at low tide."

"Really?" She surveyed the small beach, squishing her toes further in the sand. "Perfect for a little sex." Her smile was devilish.

His cock lengthened at the sight.

"Think of the sheer number of orgasms this place has seen over the years."

She stepped forward, and slipped her hands around his waist. Then into his cotton shorts to grip his ass cheeks. "Care to add a few more?"

Her hair flipped around her face, the blonde silk loose and free. Chase had finally gotten her to show her real self, and bask in it. Her rosy cheeks and glittering blue eyes nearly aquamarine in this fading light, had him in awe.

She was an angel.

"How about we add many more?"

She winked. "That confident in yourself, huh?" She moved to unzip his shorts, but he stopped her.

"I mean it. *Many* more, Samantha. Not just tonight, or this week. But really take this the full mile."

Her smile slipped.

"Will you be my girlfriend?"

She blinked. "For how long?"

"Move in with me. Make this vacation permanent."

Her hands lowered.

The silence between them filled with the rhythmic whooshes of the waves along the sand, and seagulls cawing overhead. A thousand emotions flashed across her face in that moment. An idea, a hope, a chance . . . that was quickly replaced with doubt.

"What about my job?"

"Work remotely. Or better yet, make your own career. Here."

She stepped back. As if retreating into her old self,

refusing the possibility of something new . . . with him.

He moved forward, filling the space she'd created between them.

"What are you afraid of?" he asked.

"Losing."

He blinked.

"Losing everything I've worked so hard to achieve. When I'm this close," she pinched her fingers in front of her, "to my promotion."

"You don't have to give that up. You can have both." Chase slid his hands up her arms, trying to re-establish the connection between them.

"I can't work remotely. If you're not visible, you're not considered for upper management. I have to *show up* every day."

"Samantha . . . " Her name came off his lips so easily, so lovingly, like a prayer in the wind. "Do you love your job?"

She opened her mouth to reply, but stopped short. Her silence proved the answer was no. It had been a 'yes' once, but what if she could find joy again in her new role?

"You're clinging so hard to a position you don't even enjoy." He squeezed her elbows gently. "Versus this. *Us.*"

A sheen formed in her eyes. "We've only known each other a few days . . . how can this possibly be—"

"Love?" he dared to finish. "It is for me."

Her lips parted in a quiet gasp. The glaze in her eyes thickened, which she blinked away.

"I've fallen in love with you, Samantha. Please, give us a chance."

She stepped back again, out of his reach.

His heart cinched on itself, like a rubber band squeezing its ability to beat.

After another step, she turned to move away. But she headed toward a pile of rocks poking up out of the sand.

"Samantha, wait." He lurched forward to grab her arm, to keep her from running into them, but his hand only grabbed air.

Her bare foot landed awkwardly on a rock, and she winced. Then skipped to catch herself, only to trip over another rock and land hard on her side.

She yelped as the momentum carried her over, and she threw her arm out to stop rolling. Her elbow skidded along the jagged rocks, producing a painful cry from her lips.

"Are you all right?" He moved to pull her upright, but she threw out her hand to stop him.

A nasty rash covered her palm, as well as her arm.

"Let me help you." He grabbed her wrist to help her stand, but she yanked it away.

"I'm fine!"

She shoved herself up, and winced when she put weight on her leg. Several vicious scrapes marred her knees and upper thigh.

"Jesus," he cursed himself. He reached into the bag and pulled out a bottle of water. "Show me your leg."

"Leave me alone." Sam hobbled away, back toward where they had climbed down.

"We have to rinse it out."

She finally turned and wiped at her eye. "I think we should call this a night."

Chase nearly slapped himself when he saw another scrape on her chin. A bright red tread mark thanks to the bastard rocks. And himself.

"I'm so sorry, Samantha." He stepped forward, and thumbed her cheek to get a closer look at the damage. The damage on her beautiful, perfect face.

She turned away again.

"Take me back."

"Of course." He shouldered the bag, and followed her back up to their car. She didn't wait for him to open the door for her, just threw open the thing and plopped down in the seat. And slammed the door shut.

After setting the bag in the trunk, he forced a deep breath.

So much for the most romantic night of their lives. *Please, don't let this scare her off.*

Chapter
NINETEEN

SAM'S PRIDE HURT almost as much as the scrapes from those damned rocks. Actually, a double dose of injured pride. First, from Chase basically asking her to give up her career for him to move in and play house. Second, from stumbling over the rocks and turning her into a twisted version of *Deadpool*.

"We'll get you cleaned up, take a shower, and make sure those scrapes aren't too bad, then we'll watch a movie." Chase clearly tried to sound optimistic. But the last thing she felt right now was optimism.

"No."

"No?"

"Just take me back to the rental house."

"Are you sure?"

Even *she* winced at the pain in his voice.

"Yes." She grabbed her phone from the center console, where she'd left it during what was supposed to be an evening full of mind-blowing orgasms. A real-life version of that old black-and-white film, *From Here To Eternity*, rolling around in the waves in overpowering passion.

This is what I get for thinking life is like a romance movie.

She listened to the rest of her voicemails. The first one was the computer repair guy, about her fixed laptop. She moved to the next one.

"Hey, Sam, I've got great news," her boss's voice came through crystal clear with excitement. *"I didn't want to bother you on your vacation, it's your first one in forever. But the client wanted to have the presentation today, instead of next week. Since you were still out, I asked Chuck to show them through your slides, and he read through all your talking points."*

"What the hell?" she barked aloud.

Chase glanced in her direction, his expression wary, but he remained silent.

My presentation? To Chuck? That conniving jackass who'd been trying to pilfer her clients for months. She could barely focus enough to hear the rest of the message.

"Are you ready for this, Sam? The client signed! Right then and there! You did it! Get ready for a massive payday when you come back. Enjoy the rest of your weekend, you've double earned it."

"Son of a bitch," she hissed out.

"What's wrong? The girls?"

"No, that leech stole my pitch and gave it to the client. He weaseled me out."

"Your boss?"

After a very quick recap, it took all her strength not to crush her phone in her bare hands. All the scrapes and cuts on her body didn't carry nearly the sting as this betrayal.

"Well, it is a bit of a dick move," Chase replied. "But you're all on the same team, right? Besides, there will be more deals."

The words were a bucket of ice down her back. "Are you shitting me?"

Chase blinked.

"This was the presentation I had to give to be considered for that promotion. This was *my* client, who was going to take me to the next level. And he gave it to Chuck! Do you understand what this means?"

"I think you're probably jumping to conclusions," he replied in a softer tone.

"That presentation took me a month to create. My boss knows how much this deal meant to me. He just stabbed me in the back."

Chase pulled into his driveway and put the car in park. "I know you're furious right now, but keep a rational head as you think this through."

"I need to go." She yanked on the handle and threw open the door.

Chase grabbed for her arm, pulling her back. "Wait, Samantha. It's almost midnight. We can't do anything about this right now."

She tugged her arm free, and gave him a vicious look. "When you were stewing over the city council intervening with your ASD center, I never once told you there would be other deals. That place means everything to you. I recognized that enough not to dismiss it so quickly. This *deal* was everything to me. And you just dismissed my dreams like that." She snapped her fingers. "And called me irrational for it."

He smarted back like she'd just clocked him.

Tears pricked the back of her eyes. Her limbs shook as she climbed out of the car and stormed across the yard to the rental house. All the lights were on, which proved the girls were home, and still awake.

"This is what I get for taking my first real vacation. My dreams completely shattered in the blink of an eye."

"OH SHIT!" JORDAN jumped up from the couch the second Sam burst through the door and revealed the multitude of cuts and scrapes from her date. "Please tell me the other guy looks worse."

"Trust me, he will be. I need to go back to San Francisco, now."

"Whoa, hold on a minute." Jordan followed Sam into the kitchen where she grabbed a rag to wash off her face. Which burned in so many ways. "Back up, and tell me what the hell happened. Did Chase do this to you?"

Sam scoffed and plopped down on the couch. "Of

course not. This was a fight between me, my pride, and some rocks at the beach.”

Liddy came in with the first aid kit and started pulling out bandages and antiseptic.

“Where’s Chase?” Jordan asked.

“His place. Or maybe still sitting in his car, I don’t give a shit.”

“What did he do?”

“Everything!” Sam barked. “He wants me to move in with him.”

Liddy stopped, holding the swab mid-air.

Jordan paused. “And you’re pissed by that?”

“No, well . . . yes, but only because he wants me to give up my job, and all my dreams, which are shattered now anyway. I have to get back to San Fran tonight. Salvage what I can.” She yanked back her hair, and tried to twirl it into a bun, but the tangles were too thick. “Can we just *go*? Right now!”

Jordan stopped her arm, and knelt in front of her. “Calm down. What are you talking about?”

Sam forced a shaky breath, trying to calm her frayed nerves and then told them about the voicemail from her boss. And Chase’s reaction.

She didn’t know whether to scream or cry. *How did this happen?* She’d worked tirelessly to get ahead, prove herself, put up with so much crap from her male counterparts, to show the higher-ups that she was more than capable. And poof! Gone in an instant.

For the first time all week, she regretted going on vacation.

Jordan spoke in soothing, calm tones, stroking her good side. "Sam, I'm so sorry this happened to you. There's nothing we can do right now. How about we get up early and head back in the morning, if that's what you want."

She nodded, and as Liddy finished her triage duties, they both wrapped their arms around her in a silent hug. Thank God she still had her friends.

Chapter
TWENTY

CHASE HADN'T SLEPT a wink that night. He'd sat at his kitchen island, nursing a few IPAs, along with his pride and broken heart.

He'd bared his soul to Samantha, uttered the terrifying words of *love*. And she ran.

Then he went and made an even bigger mistake in the car. He'd trivialized her response, her career, the single most important thing to her. He hadn't even realized that's what he'd done until she called him out for it.

He tossed the third empty beer bottle in the trash, hearing it shatter in the bin. "Damn that woman's temper!"

He'd picked up his phone a dozen times, to call or text. Make sure she was all right. At least from the scrapes on the beach. She'd taken quite a tumble. But he just couldn't hit the SEND button. Any time his sisters had gotten mad over the years, he'd learned they needed space to chill out. Pestering usually made things worse.

He'd give her until daylight, and approach her in the morning.

He respected Samantha too much to risk pushing her away more.

Maybe he already had.

"Put yourself in her shoes," he chastised himself. "You'd be just as pissed if they'd pulled that crap on me."

He stared at his dim reflection in the patio windows. The bags under his eyes might as well have needed their own zip code. The waters churned in the turbulent sea with an oncoming rainstorm.

A few car doors slammed in the distance, clearly from next door.

He glanced at the clock. Almost six in the morning.

He jumped up and barreled out his patio door.

From the railing, he watched Liddy carry her bags from the house to their car's open trunk. Jordan followed with her own bag.

She's leaving?

He swallowed back the panic and hurried off his deck to catch up to them.

Before she drove out of his life forever.

The second his feet hit the sand, he forced himself to go slower. He shoved his hands in his pockets, the same shorts he wore from the previous night.

Jordan turned toward him with a sympathetic look. "Mornin', Chase."

"Mornin'," he croaked back. "Is she all right?"

"You should ask her that." She gestured to the door.

"She's right inside."

"Will she even speak to me?"

"I hope so. You look like you didn't sleep much either."

He shook his head.

Liddy gave him a sad smile, and returned inside. Maybe to tell Samantha he was here. Maybe to avoid any conversation with him because she was just as mad.

"Did you mean it when you asked her to move in?" Jordan asked.

"Of course." He swallowed hard. "I love her."

"What did she say?"

"She tripped over the rocks, trying to run away."

Jordan sighed, and grimaced over her sunglasses. "That sounds like her. I'm sorry."

He glanced toward the door. Still no Samantha.

"I shouldn't tell you this, but part of this is because of her ex being a total douche. She doesn't trust romantic relationships anymore." Jordan had removed her sunglasses, and stepped closer. She crossed her arms over her chest.

"Why are you telling me, then?"

"Because I like you. And I think you're good for her. Do whatever you can to show her that."

"How can I do that if she leaves?"

She slipped her sunglasses back on. "You're smart. You'll figure it out."

"If you think I'm good for her, then why aren't you

urging her to stay?"

"Because she asked me to take her home."

Samantha finally came out the front door, her luggage rolling behind her. Her hair was pulled back again into a tight bun, pulling at the skin on her forehead. Black slacks, and a loose cream-colored top. Hints of white bandages were visible through her gauzy blouse.

Back to old Sam.

She approached him slowly, her frown so expressive it nearly ripped his heart in half again. The scrape on her face still looked vicious, but not as bright red as yesterday.

"Hey," he managed.

"Hey," she echoed, and walked right past him.

Ouch.

She shoved her bag in the car, and slammed the trunk closed.

"How do you feel?"

"Peachy."

He swallowed hard. The bitterness in her voice nearly made him wince. "Can we talk for a second?"

"I said everything I wanted to say yesterday."

"I didn't."

Samantha pursed her lips and leaned against the car. She crossed her legs, and her arms, her entire body closed off. But at least she stood still long enough for him to get the words out.

"I'm sorry for what I said. I would never trivialize or

belittle what's important to you."

"Thank you," she replied curtly. Too curt.

"I meant what I said at the beach. I love you, Samantha."

She didn't move. But he thought he caught a muscle by her temple move.

"Do you have to leave right away?"

"Yes."

"Can I drive you? So we can talk more on the way? Figure this out between us."

"I'll make this really easy on you. This week was a lot of fun, and I appreciate . . . everything." Her blush thickened across her cheeks, and then dissipated just as quickly. "But I have to return to my life. This was just a vacation. Nothing more."

Chase swallowed hard, through the abyss bottoming out in his stomach. He could read people well enough to know she'd shut him out completely already. There was no point in standing here to torture himself further.

"I'll continue to feel otherwise," he murmured. "For what it's worth, I've had the best time of my life. And I only want the best for you. I hope you chew that guy another ass at work, and go after your dreams. You deserve them."

She turned her head away, the muscles in her neck moving as she swallowed.

He took the opportunity to step forward and place the softest kiss on her cheek. Lingering to smell her hair one last time.

"Goodbye, Samantha."

SAM WANTED TO collapse on the ground and sob out her heart. Almost as much as she desired to slug the ever-loving shit out of him.

For loving her. For showing her what real romance was like. Then for ripping her soul in two.

When he'd kissed her just before she scrambled in the car and drove away with her friends in tow, that was the moment. The moment she realized she loved him back with every molecule in her body.

But it was too late. Her career was on the verge of destruction, and she had to go and save it. Avenge it.

Chew that guy another ass, he'd said.

"I intend to," she muttered out the window.

Jordan glanced in her direction. Her normally vivacious and loud friend was strangely silent as she drove through the hills along the coast.

They both deserved an apology for leaving early, but right now, she had one very important conversation to hammer out.

She grabbed her phone and dialed her boss.

Straight to voicemail.

Of course. Chicken shit.

"Hey, it's Sam. We really need to talk. I'm coming back early. I'll be in the office by ten."

She hung up.

Jordan kept her eyes on the road. "You sure you want to have that conversation today? Why not take the weekend to cool off."

"That's what I did last night."

"You never slept. That's not cooling off."

"What would you do, Jordan? If your career hung by a thread with a rival holding the scissors?"

"I would first make sure I *wanted* that job. Do you really want to continue working with people who pull that kind of shit on you?"

Her hand flew up. "That's the way the whole industry is. I'd see this wherever I went."

"You sure about that?"

"Absolutely."

Finally, Jordan looked at her. "You're not like that."

Sam stared at her.

"You expect everyone to be that way, because that's who you've surrounded yourself with. But lift your head out of the trenches for a deep breath, and I promise you'll see plenty of people who *aren't* that way."

She ground her teeth.

"That's what this week was supposed to do for you," her friend continued. "It worked, too. Over the last few days, you've really started to enjoy life again, but you allowed it to get yanked away with one bad phone call."

"A phone call that makes the rest of my *real* life

crumble around me."

Jordan frowned. "That might be an exaggeration. But I know it's important to you. So, here we are."

Speeding back to San Francisco on a cloudy day, with her friends silent. Rain pattered the windshield, and drowned out the rhythmic thumping of the road beneath the tires.

"I'm too young to have this existential midlife crisis," Sam bemoaned.

Liddy snorted from the back seat. "This is *not* a midlife crisis."

"Why do you say that?" Sam asked in the rearview mirror.

"Because you know what you want. Jordan and I already know what you want. We're just waiting for your brain to wake up and see it, too."

Chapter
TWENTY ONE

SAM STROLLED ONTO the floor of her office building at 9:45 a.m.

Jordan had smiled sadly when she'd dropped her off at home to change. But Sam had been too focused on the pending ass-chewing to address the apology she owed her friends.

A few coworkers stood from their cubicles when they noticed her walking by. She didn't make eye contact with anyone. Not yet. She beelined for her boss's office.

Chuck stood in the corner by the vending machines with a few colleagues, chuckling and shaking hands. His smug grin made her narrow her eyes.

Congratulating the man who won a pitch on someone else's work. My work.

She fisted her hand, her nails digging into her palm.

He glanced up and met her gaze. His smile widened.

She scratched her eyebrow with her middle finger, and strode by him without a word.

Her boss's door was open. His nameplate gleamed

silver in the pale office lighting: Bill Williams.

She knocked once. Hard.

Bill typed on the keyboard with two fingers, jamming the keys with an awkward expression, until he looked up from his laptop. "Sam!"

He stood, his deep-set eyes shining with excitement. He wore a plain polo shirt and dark jeans. Casual Friday.

Sam had donned her three-inch Pradas, and black suit with arctic blue blouse—to match her frigid mood. No jewelry, minimal makeup and her hair pulled back into a tight bun again. Nothing casual.

All the scrapes on her arms and her chin finally registered on his face. "What happened?"

She pushed the door closed. "Fight with a shark."

His eyebrows nearly hit his hairline. "Seriously?"

"A rare one, prone to take bites out of people's backs."

He stopped, and gave her a puzzled look. "I'm confused. What's wrong?"

He really doesn't know?

"You gave *my* presentation to *Chuck*?" His name spat off her lips like acid. Like an accusation of a crime.

He blinked. "He did great. Your pitch was *exactly* what the client wanted."

She continued glaring at him.

"I thought you'd be thrilled."

He really doesn't see that he did anything wrong.

"You thought wrong." It took all her energy not to bark

the words at him.

He sighed. "Look, I have a business to run. The client wanted the presentation this week. You know, more than anyone, we bend over backwards for their needs."

Sam shook her head. "Did you even think to ask them to wait until after I came back from vacation?"

He paused a beat. "It doesn't matter, Sam." His face changed into a forced excitement. As if he could change her mind by acting like she wasn't angry. "This means a huge paycheck for you. I know how much you wanted this deal closed, and we did it for you. We're all on the same team. We had your back."

"No, Bill." She kept her voice low. "If you had my back, you would've insisted *I* give my own presentation to *my* client."

"You mean the *firm's* client," he corrected. "You shouldn't be so upset. Everyone in that room knows you made the deal happen. You're getting the credit, too. So, stop scowling at me like I'm Brutus."

She gripped the back of a chair. "You know I needed this deal to be considered for the director role. This puts my promotion at risk."

"Sam, relax. That hasn't been decided yet. You're still in contention. *Because* you brought us this client. And the dozen before it, as well. We haven't made that decision yet."

She looked through his office window, where Chuck still laughed and high-fived his colleagues. "You haven't?"

THE WEEK HAD dragged on in misery for Chase. Nearly a whole week since Samantha had walked out, and his new mantra—patience—grew excruciatingly old.

How did it head so far south so fast?

But he couldn't sit and wallow. The ASD center was hanging by a thread. Despite the bad parting, Samantha had given him the best piece of advice he needed.

Now, he sat before the city council in a packed room. A hum buzzed through the air, and he didn't even want to count the number of phones recording behind him.

His sister sat next to him, her notecards in hand. Reese chewed on her lip. The same nervous habit she had all through her childhood. Though as an adult, she'd learned to stop before they bled.

"Will you do the talking?" she pleaded. Their mother's blue eyes looked back at him, so bright, yet unsure.

He tightened his grip on her hand. "I'll be right by your side if you need me, but this is your story. No one can tell it better than you."

She took a deep breath. "Where do I look?"

He smiled. Eye contact was always the hardest for her. "Just above their heads. Imagine a green diamond pinned to the top of their scalps."

She giggled at the reference to the video game she loved and then rifled through her notecards. They'd spent days putting together her speech, and practicing it.

The city secretary motioned for Reese to stand.

Chase had pleaded with the crotchety woman earlier in the week to get them on the agenda. She'd feigned a look of disgust, but made it happen—probably because of his long-standing relationship with half the council.

Finally, Reese stood, and nodded with the same determination she'd shown as a child when she demanded only to sit when she was damn ready. No one could rush her. She had her own pace.

Her voice trembled when she stated her name and address. "Good evening, councilmen and women. I have ASD, Autism Spectrum Disorder. I was diagnosed at two years old. I didn't speak until I was six. So, please forgive me if I stumble a bit through this. I haven't had as much practice."

A few people chuckled.

"Back then, I couldn't tell my parents why I had such anxiety around thunderstorms. I'd crouch in the corner for hours gripping my ears, because the noise was so loud." She took a deep breath, like she was reliving those moments. "Most with ASD have sensory issues. For me, I can't stand bright lights or loud noises. Which to most of the population are minor irritants, but for me, think of walking through your everyday life with an air horn blasted beside your ear drum." She fidgeted behind the podium. "Trying to concentrate in school and during tests, with fluorescent lights overhead buzzing so loud, I can't even hear myself read the question. School was the most challenging because the majority of kids still don't understand much, if anything, about ASD. They treated me as an outcast. I was alone, a lot. I wanted to play with the other kids, make friends, and have sleepovers, just like them. But I didn't know how."

Reese fidgeted at the podium, bending some of the notecards.

Chase leaned forward, ready to stand and help her. Like he'd done at countless of her therapy sessions as a teenager.

His sister soldiered on. "My family was fortunate enough to afford private care. Speech therapy, behavior therapy, occupational therapy to help me learn to write and handle my sensory issues . . . as you can imagine, councilmembers, it was a grueling schedule for nearly two decades."

Councilman Miles furrowed his brow, and a look of pain crossed his face.

Reese paused in the perfect spot. "But all those years worked. There are many more suffering from ASD than you realize. One out of sixty-eight children. All of these individuals have to grow up sometime. But as we age, we do not grow out of our disorder. Many still need significant help.

"I am extremely lucky. I live on my own, with a career that fulfills me, as a productive member of society. Which is directly related to the intervention I received as a child. I can honestly say without the help of my parents," she gestured behind her to Chase, "my brother and sister, and the financial resources, I would not be here speaking with you today, stumbling through these words. I would likely still be non-verbal, rocking in my chair, terrified of thunderstorms."

One of the councilmen wiped his eye, trying to hide it behind cleaning his glasses.

"Treatment is vital," Reese had continued. "The key is finding the right treatment program for each individual, and then being consistent with it. That's why the ASD Center like the one my brother has designed—the most advanced and comprehensive one in the country—is so crucial. People with ASD can get help from professionals. They can learn to cope with their condition, how to care for themselves, and discover job skills in a safe environment. The goal is to make every patient a functioning, happy member of society. The ultimate goal is to never have a need for centers like this one. Because everyone will be helped, and functioning on their own."

A few councilmembers nodded ever so slightly. Chase watched each of their reactions like a hawk.

"A place like this would be a dream come true for so many. Why not in Santa Cruz? Where it's already a paradise. I can't think of a more perfect setting."

She thanked the council, and returned to her seat. She gave her brother a terrified look, but Chase only beamed.

He stood and hugged her, and didn't care who watched.

Their mother would surely be crying in heaven to see her doing so well.

"I'm very proud of you." He squeezed her a little tighter, and kissed her head.

"The green diamond above their heads thing worked."

He hid a chuckle into his fist.

They sat together, and waited through more discussion and formalities.

A place like this would be a dream come true. Why not in Santa Cruz?

The words his sister recited reminded him so much of Samantha. His heart ached. If only she had felt the same way about them.

He'd resisted the urge to call her for six days. Having so much to do with his sister to get ready for this moment had helped keep him distracted. Or should he say, focused?

Miles Terrence read the motion again, and paused with a dramatic air. Councilwoman Gonzalez seconded. Miles stared at Reese as he asked the important question, "All in favor?"

Chase held his breath.

This was it. What he'd spent years of his life working on. Fighting for. What he'd promised his mother. He was all in, with everything in the balance.

The city council members raised their hands.

Every single one.

Including Miles.

"Motion is passed. Permit granted." The senior councilman smiled. "Thank you for sharing your story."

Reese jumped up and hugged her brother. "You did it!" she yelled, a little loud for the room.

Chase didn't care. "*You* did it. I always knew you could."

They stepped into the gentle breeze outside the town hall, the crowd coming out into the night air and shaking his hand. Congratulating him on his dream—his mother's dream—and promising donations for the ribbon cutting ceremony.

He should've been on cloud ninety.

Something was missing. *Someone* was missing from this night. This celebration.

He escorted his sister to her car, and kissed her on the cheek. Crickets chirped in the distance as clouds rolled across the sky.

"What are you going to do now?" she asked.

"Go home and crash, I think."

"Don't you dare crash. No car accidents tonight."

He smirked. "Very cute. Same goes for you."

"Why not go have drinks with David? Or find a girlfriend."

Chase couldn't hold back a chuckle. His sister still had no filter. "I'm working on it."

She climbed into her car and started the engine. Then rolled down her window. "Chase?"

"Yeah?"

"Mom would be really proud of you, too."

"You think so?"

"Definitely. Now, go find a girl."

As Reese drove off, Chase walked back to his car and sat in the driver's seat.

Go find a girl.

He had found one. *The* one. And she'd walked out.

He had to be patient. Patience was eating him alive, but Samantha needed more time. She needed to come to the conclusion herself that they were meant to be together. Their own personal paradise was with each other.

If she didn't . . . well, he'd write it across the sky and convince her. Bring paradise to her.

Chapter TWENTY TWO

SAM'S INTERNET WAS covered with ads for beach vacations. Each time she saw an image of the ocean, a surfer in the waves, or a sunset over a boardwalk, her heart ached.

It had been that way all week.

Chase had called several times the first few days she was gone. But she hadn't answered. She didn't know what to say.

I miss you. My body remembers you every night. Damn you for making me feel this way.

Jordan had called her the day after they'd returned to see how the conversation went with her boss. Sam had recapped it with severe doubts.

Eventually, Chase's texts had died off.

He's already moved on anyway. Why torture yourself?

She opened the news site for Santa Cruz. As if subconsciously trying to reconnect with him, even if from a distance.

The front page held a picture of Chase Bradshaw.

Her heart leapt.

He stood next to his sister, both of them smiling and holding shovels in a dirt field.

The headline flashed across her screen in large font:

New Autism Community Breaks Ground, Thanks To Local Philanthropic Family

She gasped. Then read the article feverishly.

His sister had spoken to the city council, had apparently moved the room to tears. Councilman Terrence Miles led the vote right then and there, and approved the permit.

Sam covered her mouth, her smile so wide, it hurt her cheeks.

She grabbed her phone and started a text to Chase.

Just saw the article about the ASD center. Congrats! I'm so thrilled for you. You must be so proud. I miss you. I can't stop thinking about you.

She deleted the last few lines. Too personal. Especially after she'd ignored him all week. She typed something else instead.

I'm so sorry. I overreacted. You deserve someone who doesn't lose their temper.

She huffed and deleted it again.

Please forgive me. I love you.

"Dammit," she growled, and deleted the words.

In the end, all she could send was the simple phrase *Congrats on the ASD center.*

Far too impersonal. But they were better than nothing.

She rubbed her forehead. So much pressure had taken up permanent residence at her temples in the last week. And on her shoulders. Weighing her down, and making every decision agony. Even getting out of bed each morning became next to impossible.

Because her body knew before her mind. That she loved him. But this wasn't the right time. It had never been the right time.

When her browser flashed an ad for a trip to a beach resort with a lighthouse in the background, her heart cracked.

An instant message popped up from her boss's admin, to the whole floor. "Please join us in the main lobby for a special announcement from Bill Williams."

She slammed the lid closed on her laptop.

Bill. Just looking at him made her blood boil.

She meandered to the lobby where most everyone had congregated, murmuring to each other. A hum electrified the group. She moved to the side of the room, and noticed a table with a cake box, paper plates, and plastic champagne glasses.

Pre-filled.

The tablecloth draped over the table read "Congratulations."

Her heart hiccuped. *Is this it?*

She glanced over at a few of her work friends, and they all smiled at her. One gave her a thumbs up.

Sam smiled back, and shrugged. Maybe the little talk with her boss had done some good.

Holy crap, I don't have any words prepared.

Bill approached the front of the group, a genuine smile on his face. He rubbed his hands together. "We have some exciting news to share with everyone. On the heels of closing our brand new client, we'd like to announce the new sales director."

Sam pressed her lips together, and touched her cheeks to cool the heat from her blush.

"This person has gone above and beyond," Bill continued. "And has more than earned this promotion from years of hard work. They'll carry us into our new, spectacular future . . . Chuck Holdem."

The applause from the group drowned out the rushing in her ears.

What the hell?

Chuck stepped forward, shook Bill's hand, and then waved to everyone. Bill started handing out champagne glasses, while his admin opened the cake box.

Written on top in bright red frosting, *Congrats Chuck!*

Her friends cast her confused looks, and pretended to clap, whispering to each other.

She kept her stare locked on her boss. Who clearly avoided her side of the room.

Sam turned on her heel and returned to her cubicle.

She glared at the three crystal trophies on her desk, the light bouncing off them in an array of sparkle off the wall.

Salesperson of the Year.

Three years running.

Not anymore.

A flowery perfume registered behind her just as Bill's admin tapped her shoulder, with a matching look of pity to worsen her humiliation.

With a wary smile, she said, "Bill would like to speak with you in his office, when you have a moment."

"Good thing, because he doesn't get a choice."

"I KNOW YOU'RE upset," Bill started before Sam even closed the door behind her.

"What gave it away?" she asked, each word dripping with disdain.

"Please," he gestured to the chair on the other side of his desk. "Have a seat."

She remained standing behind it.

He sighed. "I'm sorry, but I can't promote you."

"I'm almost dying to hear this excuse."

"The board felt Chuck was a better fit. I went to bat for

you in that meeting, but they disagreed."

I bet you fought so hard. She couldn't keep the thought from entering her mind. "On what grounds?"

"Honestly, you're too good in your current role."

She narrowed her eyes. "Too good? You're shutting me out because I didn't suck enough? If I had done worse, and missed my sales marks—like Chuck has—would I have been promotable then?"

He massaged the back of his neck. "You're missing the point, Sam. I can't afford to lose you in that position."

"You can't afford to keep me in that position," she corrected, her face burning as fury bubbled up from deep inside.

He sat back, and looked almost proud of himself. "Which is why I'm giving you a substantial raise."

Covering her mouth with her hand, she inhaled through her nose. "Did you ever consider that by promoting me to management, I could train people to sell and close the way I do? Essentially, replicating myself to your whole sales staff?"

Bill's lips parted and his eyes read dazed for a moment. "Sam, I don't think—"

"Let me ask this. Would you have done this if I were a man?" She leveled him a look dead in the eyes.

Bill smarted.

Sam smiled. "Thank you, for making this decision so simple for me." She spun around, flung the door open, and strolled out.

Good riddance.

The few personal belongings in her cubicle fit in her oversized purse. The same one she used to carry her laptop.

On her way out the door, she left the computer and three trophies sitting on her desk.

Out on the sidewalk, she took in her first deep, unemployed breath.

Clouds moved across the pale sky, threatening rain. The humid air pressed down on her lungs. A strong breeze blew across her cheeks. From the south.

Bringing the smell of the sea.

She walked to her car, her heels clicking on the sidewalk. With each step, more weight lifted from her shoulders. As though her heart literally floated inside her body, and carried her forward.

Sam started laughing. There was no holding it in.

This newfound freedom relieved every ounce of anxiety she'd held for days. Weeks. No, years. She could do anything she wanted. Go anywhere she pleased.

The second she started her car, there was only one place she wanted to be.

Chapter
TWENTY THREE

ARE YOU SURE you want to do this?" Ava asked, her hands on her hips.

Chase's sister had raced down from San Jose the second he called asking her to check in on his beach house for the next few weeks, while he searched for an apartment in San Francisco.

He smiled at her fierce blue eyes, all protective and determined. Just like their little sister. "Yes, I'm positive." He shoved his toiletry kit in his overnight bag.

"You've known the woman a week."

"That's all it took." He zipped up the bag, and carried it downstairs, with his sister on his heels.

"I'm thrilled you're so happy, but if you call me asking to help sell this place, I'm going to refuse with a kick in your ass."

"I won't sell. But my permanent residence will definitely change." He set the bag by the front door, with his other two rollaway bags stuffed to nearly broken zipper seams. Hopefully, his new zip code would match

Samantha's.

"Slow down for a second," Ava continued, the concern in her voice thick. "You worked so hard for this place. Most importantly, the new community is breaking ground soon. And you're *leaving?* It's not like you to be so impulsive."

If she only knew. "Which should prove just how serious I am about her." He grabbed Ava's shoulders, as if squaring her for the breaking news. "I love her. When you meet her, you'll love her, too." He held his breath. "If she'll take me back."

Ava gave the same lopsided smile that Reese used whenever her brother had teased her. "She'd be psycho if she didn't."

"Every woman gets a little psycho when she's in love. Isn't that what you told me back in high school?"

"*High schoolers* get psycho. Not grown, mature women."

He retreated to the kitchen where his laptop sat on the counter. He'd searched online to book a hotel in San Francisco, just in case things with Samantha went south. Though he prayed he wouldn't need the reservation.

"Cover the furniture with these before you leave, would you?" he asked as he patted a pile of sheets folded on the counter.

"Sure. How do you even know where she lives?"

"I called her friend, who gave me her address. Jordan seems to be rooting for me. For us to work out."

"What about the development?"

"I can manage the progress well enough from San Fran. The architects and general contractor do most of the day-to-day supervising anyway. Grand opening won't be for another year at least." He closed his laptop, slipped it in his soft briefcase, and grabbed his keys. "I hear renting beach houses to short term vacationers is popular out here." He chuckled.

She smirked.

His phone buzzed in his back pocket with a call. *David.*

"Hey, bro."

"Don't 'hey bro' me. What is this about you leaving for San Fran? If it's about the woman you met last week, you have my permission. Otherwise, the answer is hell no."

He chuckled, as he watched Ava cover his chair with a sheet. "It is. Her name is Samantha. And I think she's the one, but if not, I at least owe it to myself to find out."

David sighed over the phone line. "Okay. Gonna lose the best damn bartender I ever had."

"Not even."

"Well, get down here, say goodbye, and pick up your paycheck."

"I don't need your money."

"It's the bar's money, and yes, you do. Put it toward that center you're about to build." He could hear the smile in David's voice.

"Thanks, man. Be there in a few." He hung up. "Ava, you don't have to do that right now."

"I know, but that was David on the phone, right?" she asked as she laid the last sheet over the coffee table.

His eyebrows pulled together. "Yes."

"Then I'm coming with you." She showed all her gorgeous teeth in that smile.

He gave her an exaggerated eyeroll, and followed her out the front door.

THIS IS SO crazy," Samantha chanted to herself the entire drive to Santa Cruz. *I am so crazy.*

Eventually, she called Jordan to help reignite her confidence.

"First of all," Jordan began in her upbeat, cheerleading coach voice. "I'm so freakin' proud of you. Both for telling your boss to basically go screw himself, and secondly for going after Chase. You are so right for each other."

"God, I hope so."

"I *know* so. Did he call you?" Jordan asked, her voice shaky, like she was bouncing up and down.

"No, why?"

"No reason. Call me the second you get there. I want to make sure you're safe."

"What do I say to him? After the way I behaved?"

"It'll come to you. Just, promise me you didn't take that ridiculous muumuu with you."

Sam smirked. "Nope. I didn't bring a damn thing with

me." She pulled out the pins holding up her bun, and let her hair drape over her shoulders.

"That's what I'm talkin' about!"

"Jordan, please tell me he won't slam the door in my face."

"*Carpe diem*, Sam. Or better yet, *carpe* love."

When she pulled up to Chase's house, another car parked in his driveway. A small, yellow coupe. *Not* his car.

She forced confidence in her feet as she stepped out and approached his front door.

She rang the doorbell and glanced through the window.

Several bags sat on the faux-wood floor, the zippers nearly bursting. Sheets covered the living room furniture.

He's leaving?

Her heart sped. She pressed the doorbell several more times.

No answer. Not a sound.

She walked around to the back of the house. A few people lounged on the beach. One surfer carried his board, and dropped it on the sand beside his towel.

No sign of Chase.

She licked her lips. *Where could he be?*

He might be leaving, but from the looks of it, he hadn't left yet. Only one place she knew to try—Breakwater.

The bar hadn't started the lunch rush, so parking was easy. Sam took a deep breath and pulled the door open.

Chase leaned against the bar talking to David. A tall

woman, with mahogany curls skimming below her shoulder blades, stood beside him.

Sam's heart skipped.

He's dating someone else?

She grabbed at her chest. *So quickly?*

No. She couldn't let herself believe that. *Carpe diem, Sam. Carpe love.*

She cleared her throat.

He spun to face her. The man looked so enticing in his designer shirt and loose jeans, her knees nearly buckled. Along with her backbone.

"Samantha! What are you doing here?" he asked, his eyes wide and bright. He strode toward her wrapping his arms around her.

"I . . . " Her chest heaved, and she couldn't get a deep breath.

She looked over at the woman at the bar, a small smile on her face.

Sam's mind whirled. A rush of inexplicable emotion hit her that she couldn't decipher. She was in the arms of the man she loved, whom she thought loved her back. Yet, the niggling question in the back of her mind wouldn't let go. Was Chase going away with this woman?

"What are you doing here?" he asked again.

She swallowed hard. Then mustered the same courage that had led her down here in the first place. "I came here for you."

The handsome smile on his lips grew.

"Who's that?" she leaned in and whispered.

"Oh, Ava," he held out his hand, "com'ere."

The woman crossed the floor, standing beside Chase.

"Samantha, this is my sister, Ava. Ava, this is the woman I mentioned, Samantha."

Sam's eyes darted from Ava to Chase. "Sister?"

They both smiled at her.

Ava stuck out her hand. "Nice to finally meet you."

Sam's lip curved upward. "Nice to meet you, too." She turned her attention back to Chase. "Can we talk privately for a moment?"

Chase's beautiful smile—the one that had haunted her dreams for two weeks—shined for her. "Sure."

He pulled his car keys out of his pocket and handed them to Ava. They shared a silent message with just a glance.

"See you guys later." Ava returned to the bar.

"Talk to you later, David," Chase called to his friend.

"Have fun, you two."

He took her hand and led her out the door. Before she could collect her thoughts, he spun around and clasped her face, bringing her in for a kiss.

Her hands gripped his arms, sinking into those delicious lips, praying she'd never have to go another day without them.

He backed away a few inches. "I'm sorry." He inhaled. "I'm sorry for not supporting you like you supported me. I minimized how important your job was to you. And that hurt you. It'll never happen again."

Her breath caught in her throat. The sincerity in his words warmed her heart, and left her speechless. She believed him. "Apology accepted," she whispered.

"Please, tell me what happened with your boss. The promotion?"

She shook her head, in disbelief that she couldn't have cared less about those two jerks at her former employer. Her former job. What was once her entire life just a day before. "It's time for a change. I can tell you all about it, but, Chase," she braced herself for the worst, "I went by your house. All your furniture is covered. Are you leaving?"

His expression guarded, he replied, "I was coming to see you."

Her eyebrows lifted. "For how long?"

He kept his eyes trained on her as he took her hands. "As long as you'd have me."

She blinked. *Wow! He didn't give up on us.*

When she hadn't said anything, he continued. "I was going to look for an apartment. Maybe I'd keep my place here." He shrugged a shoulder. "Or rent it out. I don't know for sure. What I do know is that I missed you, and we belong together."

She smiled as the most incredible feeling flooded her body. God, she had so much she wanted to tell him. "Here." She pulled her car keys out of her purse, handing them to him. "Let's get out of the sun, and go somewhere."

As he steered her vehicle onto the road, he glanced her way. "Your hair is down."

She smoothed a hand over her locks, enjoying the refreshing change. "I think it will be a long time before I wear a bun again." She grinned. "I quit my job. I'm going to create my own level-up, and refresh my career. It took me a week away from everything to realize that."

To see who truly valued me and my goals, not just for their own gain.

"What happened?"

"Just as a I expected. The company signed the client on my presentation. But Chuck was awarded the promotion. They said I was too valuable to promote, and they tried to offer me a raise instead."

His face scrunched like he swallowed raw squid. "That doesn't make sense. Well, I'm sure it did to your boss—"

"Ex-boss."

He grinned. "Right. But that's extremely short-sided. I mean, look where they are now. Minus their best sales rep."

"Exactly. It's rather liberating. I don't know if they'll learn anything from this, but at least I stayed true to myself. The money was good for a while, and I learned a lot. But I was getting burned out. I was a cash-cow to some, a fragile woman to others." She took a calming breath. "So, when all this came to a head, I cut bait. And I have you to thank, partially."

He lifted a brow in amusement. "Partially?"

"Well, Jordan and Liddy too, since the vacation was their idea. This break, with no care in the world, taught me what I was missing. I had to come to the conclusion on my own, but—"

"After two long weeks." He feigned disbelief.

She inclined her head. "Yes, so thank you for your patience."

When the car stopped, she instantly realized their surroundings. "We're at your place?"

He rested a hand on the back of her seat and faced her. "Two damn weeks, Samantha."

Her tummy did a funny little flip.

Without giving her a chance to respond, he slipped out of the car, and swung around to her side. Holding her hand, he led her into his house.

"You were really coming to find me in San Francisco?" she asked once she laid eyes on the covered furniture.

"Yup." He slipped her bag off her shoulder and set it on the kitchen counter behind them. He wrapped his arms around her.

"But what about the center?" She spun in his arms, looking up into his gorgeous blue, smiling eyes.

"I'd planned on managing it from there. I'm sure I'd make a few trips back here, get some surfing in, too, while I'm at it." He shrugged a shoulder. "But I'm prepared to do whatever it takes."

Her hands slid up his biceps to his face. She stroked his stubble with her fingertips. "I can't believe you were going to do that."

"Your dream was important to you."

It was that simple. She couldn't believe she'd walked away from such a caring, generous man two weeks prior.

She lifted on her toes to kiss him sweetly. "I have new dreams now."

He smiled. "God, I can't believe you're here."

"Believe it. I've fallen in love with you." She gripped the sides of his face and crushed her lips against his.

He tipped his head through their hungry, passionate embrace, pulling her closer.

She moaned, circling her arms around his neck, clinging desperately.

His ardent erection pressed against her.

"Samantha," he breathed over her lips.

She sucked in air as he laid kisses down her neck. His hands gripped her ass pulling her closer.

She whimpered from the longing he caused her body to feel.

"Chase," she whispered.

He ravished her with his affection. "Samantha, I can't wait another second."

Neither could she. She pulled her blouse over her head and flung it across the room.

Chase's lips crashed down on her newly exposed skin.

Pulling on her bra straps, his mouth captured one nipple, lapping and tugging.

She bowed her back, begging him for more. She fumbled with his shorts' button and zipper.

He unclipped her bra and dropped it at his feet. Then finished the job on his shorts before retrieving a condom from his back pocket.

"Turn around, Samantha. Lean over the back of the sofa."

Oh, she knew just what he wanted, and she trembled in anticipation.

His hands caressed her thighs, reaching beneath her skirt to gain access to her ass.

"Samantha, I had a fantasy of hiking up your skirt," his movements followed his words, "and taking you over your office desk."

Her breath hitched.

His fingers hooked under her thong and dragged the confection to the floor. With her skirt bunched at her waist, he continued massaging and caressing her ass and hips, slowly inching his way to the center. "From now on," his finger slid through her wet crease, "we go through all the ups and downs of life together. Right, Samantha?"

Oh heavens. She couldn't think. "Yes," she breathed.

A finger pushed into her channel.

She mewled.

"That's right." He leaned over her body. "Because that's

what people do when they're in love. They take care of each other, support each other, share their dreams."

His ministrations sped, and a climax buried deep inside began its slow ascent to the surface.

He pulled out his finger and slowly pushed into her with his cock. He groaned. His arms wrapped around her, enveloping her with his strong, warm body. His lips kissed her neck, up to her ear. "And I do love you, Samantha."

"I love you, Chase," she panted. "I didn't want to, but you filled my thoughts, my heart . . . every cell of my body."

"Samantha." His voice turned breathless.

"Unh." Her orgasm escalated to its maximum strength. She cried out his name. She was vaguely aware of his release with a growl.

Holding her tight, he slipped out of her and took them to the floor. Lying on the soft green rug—the same one she'd imagined them making love on when they first met—they panted for several moments before she turned in his arms.

She stared into his sparkling eyes, amazed at how her life had changed so dramatically in just a few weeks.

"What are you thinking," he asked softly.

"I never knew it could be like this."

He smiled and wagged his brows. "Oh yeah, and I'm just getting warmed up."

She smacked his chest. "I mean . . . you and me . . . being together." She couldn't find the words to express the depth of what she felt.

He rolled her on her back and covered her body with his, their skin searing together with the promise of more. "Sweetheart, we have a lifetime to perfect 'you and me'. And I can't wait."

But wait! There's more! Check out **Hot Spell** and read all about Jordan.

Sneak Peak
HOT SPELL
Chapter 1

JORDAN WINCED AS Liddy grabbed the mini snow globe off the dresser—the one Frank had bought her on their lovers' getaway to San Diego—and threw it at the wall. The trinket shattered into a million pieces and tiny shrapnel flew halfway across the room.

"Ugh!" her friend bellowed, and slumped down on the end of her bed. "What a prick!" Soon the huffs of anger turned to sobs.

Jordan grabbed tissue box off Liddy's nightstand before the snot from her nose dropped onto the carpet. "Here." She handed a fresh tissue to her friend. "That snow globe didn't go with the rest your collection anyway."

Tears streamed down Liddy's cheeks from her red, swollen eyes. She looked like hell. "I just can't believe it." *Blow. Sniffle.* "I really thought he was the one."

Jordan glanced at Sam to see her eyes roll. Translation, *how many times have we heard that line?*

Sam rubbed her back. "I know."

Blow. Sniffle.

"Things were going so well between us," Liddy choked out.

Well, it appears not. Jordan didn't mean to be cold, but how many of Liddy's breakups had they endured?

Lydia Michelle Drake was a sweetheart. Truly kind and fun-loving, but clingy as shit. After a few months—sometimes weeks—men caught whiff of her clinginess and high-tailed it out of there. Kudos to Frank for lasting six months.

"Sweetie, do you want some hot tea?" Jordan asked.

"Sure." *Sniffle. Blow.*

"Sam, give me a hand, would ya?"

Samantha followed her into the kitchen, and they started their routine of making tea. They'd pulled this ritual often enough, they knew where everything was.

"It's different this time, Jordan," Sam observed. "She's taking it a lot harder."

"I know. Probably because Frank stayed with her for so long," Jordan whispered back.

"We gotta fix this."

"Hell, if I know what to do," she replied as she dug out the creamer.

They worked side-by-side in silence. Sam found scones and set them on a platter. Jordan brought down plates and cups from the cabinet.

"I got it," Sam said with a smile on her lips.

"What?"

"A vacation."

Jordan tapped her lips, the gears grinding in her mind.

"Let's go somewhere. Get her the hell out of here. Change of scenery and all that."

"Yeah, that could work." The words came out slowly. "It's been almost a year since our last vacation."

"Yup. Worked wonders for me. Got me out of my funk."

"Not that you would admit it at the time," Jordan said with a grin.

"Okay, Miss Priceline, go work your magic. Find us a good deal to go somewhere."

"Where are you thinking, Florida? Or New York for a girl's weekend?"

Sam hesitated. "No, I think we need farther. Like, out of the country."

Jordan nodded. The thoughts already brewed on high steam.

JORDAN HAD A mission as she booted up her computer: find a fix for Liddy's broken heart. A good distraction could help her sweet, naive friend realize she and Frank weren't meant to be forever.

Speaking of which, when was her last, er, distraction? This vacation could be good for her, too.

The usual column of ads populated the right side of her screen. She immediately went to her favorite discount vacation site. A few images of Mexican beaches quickly popped up. She typed in the search bar.

I wonder if Europe is on sale this time of year.

She scrolled down the page. Way too many zeros involved. *Okay, perhaps we won't be going* that *far away.*

Maybe Australia. *Wait, isn't it winter there now?*

She opened another site—more ads for Mexico.

"All right, all right," she told the computer.

She clicked on the various deals: Cozumel, Cancun, *oh,* Puerto Vallarta. *Now isn't that a great looking resort?* The all-inclusive property shaped in a big U was situated right on the ocean. They flouted a private beach, several pools, bars and restaurants, a nightclub, spa packages, and shuttle service from the airport.

"Puerto Vallarta it is," she said to no one.

She'd been to Mexico a few times; it was a relatively easy trip from San Francisco. Never been to Puerto Vallarta.

Although she could see the Latin in her dark brown eyes, olive skin, and brown wavy hair every time she looked in the mirror—she didn't speak much Spanish. All the Latin blood came down from her father's side. Retired military, her dad had instilled his intense work ethic in Jordan at an early age.

School was out for the summer, and her coaching duties for high school cheerleading camp weren't for another six weeks. Sam ran her own online software firm, and could manage it from anywhere, even across international borders.

The only real question was Liddy. Could she get the time off from her retail job? Would she even try, with how reclusive she tended to be after a breakup?

Jordan glanced across the room, at her various gymnastics trophies and plaques. The bronze medal dangled from the arm of one trophy, from the Olympic trials her senior year in high school. She'd missed her final vault, and lost her spot on the official team . . . by three tenths of a point.

She stood, stretched out her muscles and touched the floor, keeping her legs straight. Her ACL protested. It was an old injury, but sitting too long exacerbated it.

She picked up her phone and shot a text to Sam.

Get your passport. Puerto Vallarta awaits.

Sam replied quickly. *Ole!*

Jordan smiled and dialed Liddy's number.

"Hello?" Her friend sighed, so depressed in her quiet, monotone voice.

"Hey sweetie. How are you doing today?"

Another sigh, longer than the first. "I'm alright."

Not likely. "Well, you will be. Let's get away. I found a great deal for us at an all-inclusive resort. We leave next week."

"Oh, I remember you guys talked about it, but I don't know, Jordan . . ."

"Baby, you sound like crap, which means you feel like crap, which means your work is like crap." She exhaled. "Ask your boss. I bet Bernie would be thrilled to have you take a week off. C'mon, it'll be good."

"I'll ask, but don't book anything until I know for sure."

"Call me back."

They disconnected and before Jordan could get back from her kitchen with a green smoothie, Liddy replied.

I can't believe it. He said take as much time as I need.

"That's my girl." Jordan spun in her seat to face her screen. "Beautiful Mexico, here we come."

A Message
FROM THE AUTHORS

Thank you so much for reading!

If you enjoyed this story, please consider posting a review at one or more of your favorite retailers, as well as GoodReads. Even a short review, one or two lines, can be a tremendous help and encouragement to the authors. Your review is also a gift to other readers who may be searching for just this sort of story, and will be grateful you helped them find it.

Thank you!

Mia London & Susan Sheehey

About THE AUTHORS

Mia London

Mia London loves to write.

After reading fiction for years, she decided it was finally time to put those images and scenes floating around in her head down on paper.

She is a huge fan of romance, highly optimistic, and wildly faithful to the HEA (happily ever after). Her goal is to create a fantasy you will enjoy with characters you could love.

She lives in Texas with her attentive, loving, supermodel husband, and perfectly behaved, brilliant children. Her produce never wilts, there are no weeds in her flowerbeds, and chocolate is her favorite food group.

www.Facebook.com/MiaLondonAuthor

Twitter- @MiaLondonAuthor

Webpage- www.MiaLondon.com
Email- mia@mialondon.com

Susan Sheehey

Susan Sheehey writes contemporary romance and romantic suspense adventure. Water plays a crucial element in all her novels, and she's a strong advocate for Autism awareness and acceptance. She squeezes in writing time between chauffeuring around her two boys, and guzzling down French Vanilla coffee. Her beloved husband keeps her relatively sane, and full of laughter. She and her family live in Texas.

www.SusanSheehey.com
www.Facebook.com/SusanSheehey
www.Twitter.com/SusieQWriter
www.Pinterest.com/SusanSheehey

Join her newsletter for monthly announcements, updates, ARC requests, and special giveaways!

https://landing.mailerlite.com/webforms/landing/p5b0i9

www.ingramcontent.com/pod-product-compliance
Lightning Source LLC
Chambersburg PA
CBHW031957180726
48283CB00008B/2464